The Unmasking of the Truth

By Bayley Seton

ISBN 978-1-66787-282-7

To Monica, Siobhan, Omar Bradley, and the memory of Liam. May Luna leave you in peace to find your bonds with each other. And to Moira, you deserved better.

Last, but not least, to DM and SM – *my best poems.*

*"A metaphor is a kind of magical changing room —
where, one thing, for a moment, becomes another,
and in that moment is seen in a whole new way. As
soon as something old is seen in a new way, it
stimulates a torrent of new thoughts and
associations, almost as if a mental floodgate has
been lifted."*— Mardy Grothe

Think back to your 8th grade English class. Perhaps an
older woman or man, standing at the front of an
overcrowded and stuffy room, trying to desperately to
manage a group of energetic thirteen-year-olds, squirming
in their seats in resistance to the delights of *The Red Badge
of Courage.* Wearily, the teacher writes "M-E-T-A-P-H-
O-R" on the board and steps back expectantly. Yes, this is
going to be on the test. Yes, you have to know it.

From the Greek: *metaherein,* to transfer. A figure of
speech which uses one thing to represent something
symbolic or essentially true about another. A predominant
form in fiction: that is, a story which conveys an essential
truth without corresponding to anything we see in the
world. *A mask which both points to and obscures the real.*

The story that is told in these pages is not the story of
any particular family: the Quinn family does not exist in
life, but if you pull the away the mask, the essential truth
of their story does....

Part One -- The Golden Garbage Truck

"The secret of every great fortune, when there's no obvious explanation for it, is always some forgotten crime." Honoré de Balzac

It begins with a garbage truck, unusual perhaps, but there it was -- the linchpin of all that followed. For Billy at least, and certainly for those around him, the truck, an Imperial 5000, was the instrument of change. Now, you may be thinking about the irony of this: a vehicle that collects the detritus of other people's lives creating change, but if you think like that, this is not the book for you. "Irony" and "detritus" are lofty concepts. This is a story of ordinary people, and frankly, as we will see, ordinary predators. But we digress.

Billy was new to his job as a Sanitation Inspector, having only been promoted some six weeks previously. This was a cold morning in late fall, close to the holiday season, too cold for him to have only his white boss shirt on without a jacket, but he loved the way its crisp white starched collar and polished brass badge made him stand out from the average sanitation worker in their grubby overalls.

The truth was that Billy had never thought of himself as a boss, and still really didn't. A city job, he told his children, was "welfare for the working man": an opportunity to grab some union benefits, enjoy a relatively relaxed working environment (read: hide from your boss all day) and ease into a cushy retirement. He had been content to work as a basic laborer without ever taking the Civil Service tests that would lead to promotion, but his wife Moira would not let up, nagging and nagging until finally he approached the shop steward to ask about the test.

"It's easy, breezy," the shop steward said, barely containing his mirth, "just take this here guide and memorize all the questions and answers." Billy looked despairingly at the thick booklet, deciding it was worth trying, if only to shut Moira up. Besides, it might be easier still to ride around bossing crews. He carried the booklet with him everywhere, reciting the questions and answers to himself in a low whisper. Like memorizing the Catechism at Mary, Queen of Angels Orphanage where he grew up.

The first test was a disaster, with Billy scoring barely in the 20s. Not long after, the shop steward took him aside. "So, how'd youse make out?" he asked. Billy was embarrassed to admit how poorly he had done, but annoyed that he had wasted so much time on a losing cause. "I memorized it like you said…question 1, A, question 2, D…" he stopped when the steward burst out laughing. "You an idjit? They change the order! You can't memorize like that! What the question SAYS and what the answer SAYS! Christ on a cracker!" He walked away, shaking his head and laughing.

Far from discouraging him, the answer made Billy determined to try again. When the test came up again, six months later, Billy had done it. Studying constantly, the *words* this time, not the letters and numbers. He knew the content cold. It was only later when he scored an almost perfect 98 that the city realized it had to rotate the questions. No matter, he was in.

Being a supervisor was a bigger problem. Working on a crew made it easy for him to skate by as "one of the guys." Now he was on his own, and it was impossible to blend into a background. Nor did he have any idea what following the rules looked like. At the orphanage, and later in the series of the foster homes that followed, and still later in life, he listened closely to the siren-song of his own wants and desires, masking his rebellion with denials, and a vague stupefied look.

Food was often an issue in The Home, and Billy was always hungry; and his hunger would remain stamped on him until the end of his life, in a variety of ways from his small stature to emotional approach to life. Asking for more was sure to provoke a rebuke, a stinging slap on the cheek or a smack across the palm with a wooden ruler. Who was Billy to suggest that his needs were not being met through the generosity of God and the benevolence of the Sisters? Early on then he had learned that the simplest course was to take what he needed from someone whose back was turned, or a younger, smaller child who couldn't complain. When consequences loomed beyond a simple slap, Billy learned to paint his face in a picture of stupefaction, his blank face and slack jaw carefully practiced leaving observers shaking their heads in pity. It wasn't enough however to escape the label that they would pin on him – "retarded." While he knew the name should have stung as much as the ruler, Billy didn't mind. It became the mask he could hide behind and still get what he wanted.

Billy's new inspection district was most of the South Bronx, an area that in the 1980s had seen arson, violence, and high crime rates. Most of the city workers who were assigned to the area viewed it with fear and suspicion, traveling in and out as quickly as possible to avoid trouble. For many of the sanitation crews who worked there, this was a boon. Supervisors stayed away, allowing them to roam or hide at will. They grabbed tips from restaurants wanting to skip the high fees of the commercial carting companies, or the isolated homeowners with bulky garbage to throw away. It also meant more time to rifle through garbage for interesting swag, or to load the bottom of the truck, not compact it and take off early for the dump. This last work evasion strategy, however, was the one the City had decided to address.

Shortly before Billy's promotion, a new Mayor had taken office. Horton Jackson Lee, "Hootie" to his friends, was himself a former sanitation worker who rode his status as an average Joe to public office, proudly proclaiming that he would, winking significantly, "clean up" the city. Hootie had ridden a truck himself in this very area, learning all the tricks for dodging work and puffing the pension. Overwhelmed by the demands of his new job, Hootie decided to focus on the thing he understood – making those lazy sanit workers, and their powerful union, respect his new position. Speaking at the main sanitation garage on 10th Avenue, Hootie proclaimed that he was announcing a new program, "Hootie's Hundred," a set of 100 rules that all crews had to follow. Over the loud grumbling of the rank and file, he also proclaimed that the new rules came with an incentive to the supervisors who had to enforce them – an automatic 50-point bonus for an Inspector writing five citations on the next-up promotion test for Area Inspector, virtually a guarantee of promotion to anyone smart enough to write their name, which Billy had clearly mastered.

Billy dreaded getting the crews to listen to him but finding a way to screw them and advance himself was easy. Remembering his purpose, he stepped from his white Inspector's car and nervously adjusting his clip-on tie, approached the cab of the truck. As he walked up, he could see the driver, Skeeter-Breath Capolino, watching him in the side mirror, one gorilla-hairy arm dangling out the open window. Skeeter was legendary for his ability to milk any situation to his advantage. Facing him on street-level would have been daunting enough, but it was clear that Skeeter had no intention of ceding any advantage and fully intended to use the height of the cab and the noise of the engine to make this difficult.

"Good morning!" Billy ventured. "Yeah, I need to take a look to see how full you are…"

Snorting, Skeeter yells, "Be my guest, boss man."

Billy walks to the back of the truck. Technically, it was a violation for Skeeter Breath and his partner Weak Willy to not come around to the back with him, but he wasn't ready to argue this too. The truck engine is percolating with a diesel rattle as Billy reaches the hopper basket. Mixed refuse filled the bin, loose food, garbage not in bags – just the kind of garbage that a restaurant would tip to have carted away. That was also a clear citation. Weak Willy should have engaged the hopper blade pulling the garbage up into the main bay before getting up into the cab. Riding around with a hopper bin full of garbage was

7

a recipe for a trail of garbage spilling out onto the street, along with a string of neighborhood complaints. It could also mean that the crew was going to tip a half-full truck at the end of the shift. Another citation. Billy leans in over the reeking mess to get a closer look. His position is awkward because he is short, and because he is being careful not to rub his clean uniform on the stinking edges of the truck refuse bin. His center of gravity tips as he leans, slipping and pitching head-first into the bin. As he falls, Billy grabs futilely for the side wall, hitting what the Sisters would have called his "rock head" on the hopper blade. In the cab Skeeter Breath hears the loud thump. Quinn ain't so bad after all, he thinks to himself, believing it is Billy knocking on the side of the truck to indicate that he could move on. Skeeter engages the hopper arm with a lever on the dashboard, pulling the garbage up inside the truck. Billy faints as the arm moves towards him.

Sometime later, Billy wakes to find himself lying on a bed of slimy trash in the semi-darkness. The truck is rocking slightly back and forth as it travels at speed on a highway, headed for (Billy guesses) the Great Kills dump. Overhead, a dim, grimy light is filtering in through the top vent slits. Billy yells futilely knowing that they won't hear him over the shake and rattle of the engine. He is thankful that Skeeter hasn't engaged the compactor arm (a citation though, as the truck is only half-full.) His head aches where it hit the hopper blade and reaching up, he can feel dried blood along his face and neck. He can also see that it has cascaded down onto the clean white of his shirt. Moira will be mad at him, he thinks.

It can't be long though before they arrive at Great Kills, the huge dump on Staten Island. Skeeter will be sure to engage the compactor arm before they arrive, he reckons, crushing him against the back wall of the truck. It will be sure to catch him and pin him. His recent promotion test is still firmly imprinted in his mind. Question: what is the most frequent cause of truck fatalities? Answer: being crushed by the compressor arm after falling into the garbage bay. He wonders vaguely what a line of duty funeral will look like for a Sanitation Inspector. Will there be bagpipes? He is distant from the idea of his own impending death, but drifts into a stupor imagining a giant nun yelling at him for the fires he set in the dormitory.

Again, time passes. With a bump the truck comes to a stop. Billy knows that they have arrived at Great Kills and he waits for the compressor arm to pulverize him. Instead, with a great screeching jolt, the bed of truck tilts upwards, spilling Billy and a mound of trash on top of him. He claws his way to the surface of the mound in time to witness the truck receding in the distance. Exhausted, he collapses backwards onto the mountain of garbage. A group of gulls circles overhead in the afternoon sun, idly dumping a warm bit of guano in his general direction. Smiling, he thinks back to a Disney movie he has seen. Pinocchio and Gepetto on a raft, trapped inside the whale Monstro. They struggle to paddle their way out but are trapped. Finally, the whale sneezes and they are propelled out onto the ocean. Sheer dumb luck, he thinks. Just like Pinocchio.

This was the day that changed everything.

At the approximate time that Billy was walking towards Skeeter's truck, his wife Moira was sitting down to her second cup of coffee in her kitchen. The family lived in a small waterfront house in a forgotten backwater of Brooklyn called Gerritsen Beach that had progressed from mill to mansion to veteran's development to middle class escape in a cycle that reflected the rest of the borough's cultural change. Known as the "Irish Rivieria" to locals who began buying up and expanding the resort-style bungalows in the 1950s, the house had come with a dock on the Plumb Beach inlet that made Billy feel as if he was entering a new stage of social acceptance. Over the 20 years that they had lived in the house, they had worked hard at saving and expanding it through a variety of maneuvers from second jobs to bargaining with neighbors for help with expansions. Their older children, Moira Ellen (but known by her middle name, Siobhan), Liam, Jr. (known as Liam – he hated being called Billy), and Monica, had grown and were out of the house already, leaving only the youngest school-age children, Omar Bradley, and Luna Lynn still at home.

Moira was not sitting at the table at this moment because she was idling. On the contrary, she worked her entire life just as hard, if not harder than Billy. No, she was sitting and reflecting on how she had arrived at this moment with perhaps a insight that her family had always found eerie: there was a change coming, she was sure. Her marriage to Billy had brought her children that she loved dearly, or at least mostly, and more material things, such as the house, than she had originally expected, but there was a sadness too at this moment as if there was a grief that had not yet grown into itself, because it drifted without an object.

If the truth was told, as Moira would say in old age, they made an odd couple. Billy was small for a man, barely standing 5'5" and Moira was tall for a woman, over 5'10", an odd picture when they stood together. Nor were they well matched in wits, as many had noted over the years. Billy had struggled in school, reading well enough but not able to reason his way to any but the most outlandish conclusions. Moira had excelled in her vocational high school but also took a disciplined approach to reading whatever came her way including newspapers, magazines, and books from the local library. She was a careful and charismatic listener who made good tips as a waitress because of her ready laugh and quick wit. Yet their mutual and unconventional childhood had one element of common ground – no father in sight. Moira and her sister Monica had been raised by a single mother.

Moira had met Billy at the candy store he owned with his brother in Canarsie. She had grown up not too far away, her mother sinking into a bitterness that knew no bounds after the hit and run death of her husband. From an early age Moira had scrambled to lug the heavy ashcans and clean the apartment corridors of the buildings her mother managed. She was used to hard work, but longed for something of her own. Billy seemed sure to provide a steady presence, as he longed for a family too of his own. After their marriage, and the birth of two children in rapid succession, the truth turned out to be somewhat different than Moira had expected. Billy never really connected with the children or her in any meaningful way, as if they were accessories to a life he had imagined, a source of possible entertainment but not worthy of any genuine notice. Often gloomy or absent, his kids thought of him as the "crank" whose irrationality and anger would spring abruptly from the most innocent of triggers. He talked loudly and often about the importance of family, especially when it was a way to manipulate them, but Moira worried that there was no real connection between them, that they were no more real to Billy that the furniture that surrounded him.

Time and again too, Billy made choices in those early years that were impulsive, risky even. There was the

11

time he was teaching her to swim in a lake upstate. Moira's time as the child of her widowed mother didn't lead to much time to idle on the beach or at a public pool. As a result, she had never learned to swim. This was puzzling to Billy, who insisted that she had to learn. He taught her the way he had taught his young children – standing in waist deep water, forcing her face down and pulling her towards him by the hair. The painful result was that they all learned to swim painfully, if nothing else to avoid the hair pulling. But Billy also liked to test their ability by catching them off guard.

Moira had spent the morning with Billy and the kids in waist deep water, Billy pulling her along as she practiced swimming. Now they had walked to the end of a long dock, to look into the deeper water before going for lunch. Moira had a headache from all the hair pulling, was embarrassed at having to learn to swim so late in life and was convinced that Billy was enjoying the swimming lessons way too much. When Billy lured Moira to the end of the dock, pointing down into the water at some sight only he could see, she was distracted and anxious to get back to their campsite. Moira unsuspectingly leaned slightly over to look as well. With a smirk, Billy stepped behind her, sweeping her legs away and pushing on her upper body. She sank like a stone, her feet sinking into the soft bottom of the lake. With dismay, she tried to pull her feet out, simultaneously pulling with both arms towards the surface. Through the clear water, Moira could see Billy on the dock laughing and looking down at her. She saw him gesturing to others, not for help but to look down at her in delight. She tried waving her arms, but he only laughed harder and waved back. She focused desperately on tried to pull her legs out of the deep mud with both hands, blackness gathering at the edges of her vision.

She came to lying on her side on the dock, vomiting lake water on a stranger whose street clothes were all wet. The wood of the dock was rough and hot in comparison to the lake water. The man leaned over her, urging her to "take some deep breaths and relax" before turning angrily to Billy. "What is wrong with you?" he shouted, "she could have died." Billy waved dismissively, "she was ok," he said, "you over-reacted." The man helped Moira to her feet and walked slowly alongside her as she left the dock. This story would be retold over the years by the family, each of them shaking their heads in complicit disbelief but acceptance. "Whatta you gonna do?" They asked themselves. "That's your father."

As the older children began attending school, Moira went to work in a series of waitressing jobs that allowed her to be home in time for the children's return from school. She loved these jobs not just for the extra money they provided (and which she carefully hid in a jar in her pantry), but also for the interaction with the customers, the jokes, the banter, and political discussions that were as much a part of her day as the plates of eggs or spaghetti that she carried. It was at one of these diners that she met Harvey Goldfarb, an older accountant who liked to stop for a coffee and pie on his way home.

Harvey was an elegant middle-aged bachelor, tall and thin with a sprinkling of salt and pepper at his temples and deep brown eyes. Filling in for another waitress one day on the afternoon shift, Moira noticed him immediately sitting at a window booth at Dino's Dinner in Sheepshead Bay. He was intent on a newspaper crossword puzzle on the Formica table in front of him, working it with a fountain pen and smiling in vague amusement. Over the next few meetings their relationship progressed from casual teasing to discussions of politics and philosophy. Gradually Moira came to deeply appreciate Harvey for his kind-hearted view of the world, his wit and sense of humor, and especially for the intense way he listened to her.

And then came Moira's moment of epiphany. A single moment of clarity that reshaped her understanding of all that came before and afterwards. It changed the way

Moira understood her relationship with Billy, as well as her understanding of his demands and their consequences. On June 19, 1953, everything changed for Moira.

Over the weeks and months before, Harvey and Moira had spent every spare moment discussing the trial and conviction of Julius and Ethel Rosenberg, the so-called "atomic spys." The tabloids had been filled with the salacious details of the investigation and trial, the narrative building to its own critical mass of claustrophobic betrayal and anger: a domestic drama transported to a national stage, with deadly consequences.

For Harvey, the trial pointed to a deep-seated anti-Semitism, along with a rush to justice against an already marginalized community. Moira saw only a young mother of children, caught up in her husband's selfishness and stupidity, a selfishness that could only lead to the destruction of the entire family. As much as she tried, Moira found it increasingly difficult not to read her own story into the Rosenberg's saga of manipulation, carelessness and treachery.

Moira was not scheduled to work at the diner on June 19, the day that the Rosenbergs were to be executed but she was at the candy store alone from early in the morning, since Billy had announced that he was driving up to Sing-Sing to stand outside the prison and wait for the announcement that "the Commies were dead." He explained gleefully that it would be a circus, and that he couldn't wait. Moira was sickened by his reaction, and annoyed that that she would be left alone all day to manage the store. In the late afternoon, Harvey showed up. It was the first time that he had ever visited the candy store, but he sat at the counter with a wry smile as if it was routine for him. "Black coffee with an ice cube and pie," he said, as if she didn't know already.

Harvey remained at the counter the rest of the afternoon, sipping his coffee and eating several slices of pie. When Billy didn't return to help with the evening rush, he donned an apron, coming behind the counter to serve customers while she organized the kid's supper. By early evening they were alone in the store, silently listening to the news on the radio in the hope of a last-minute reprieve. Then the word came, "Breaking News, Julius and Ethel Rosenberg are dead..." Moira moved to snap off the radio with the especially devastating news that it had taken five jolts of electricity to kill Ethel Rosenberg, the last administered after she had been taken from the chair presumably dead but had been found to be still alive.

Moira began to sob. Reaching for her hand, Harvey said "come with me and bring the kids."

In the weeks that followed Moira lapsed into a deep depression, claiming illness and laying on the couch all day. She tried to work it out in her mind. She knew she didn't want to leave Billy, especially as it was hard to articulate what had changed. Harvey was a good man, but she had realized that her feelings, particularly considering Ethel Rosenberg's death, went deeper than a choice between two men. Ethel Rosenberg was a pawn, she thought, caught between political forces she couldn't control. Worse than that, she had died because of her husband's careless disregard for the impact of his decisions on his family, and because of her brother's casual implication of her in something that she didn't even know about. Worse still, she had left behind two sons that meant the world to her. Leaving Billy would not solve her problem, and perhaps nothing ever would. The only solution for Moira was to stay where she was, close to her children and to find something for herself, not a relationship necessarily, but a meaning that would help her move beyond Billy's petty selfishness.

In the intuitive way of many selfish people, Billy sensed that something had shifted in his relationship with Moira, but he misunderstood the nature of the choice she had made. Later, he would tell his adult children that Moira had decided to leave him for another man, but that the man wouldn't accept the children. In this telling, Billy was all victim, and Moira wasn't enough of a prize encumbered as she was with three kids. When Moira became pregnant again some months later, he saw the baby who was born (a girl named Luna) as his personal prize – evidence of both his virility and his trophy for reclaiming his wife.

Moira was contemplating some of this as she sat drinking coffee on the morning that Billy disappeared in the maw of the truck. Years had gone by, she had bid Harvey a wistful goodbye and her family had grown by yet another child, her youngest son, Omar Bradley. Yet she still hadn't found that elusive something that would help her move on. It was at that moment that the phone rang.

Moira rose from her place at the table and answered the phone.

"Moira?"

"Hi, Doozy. Billy's not here, he's at work." Doozy Moran was the dispatcher at the Zerega Ave Garage. Though her real name was Dorothy, everyone called her Doozy because everything about her was so over the top. Moira had known her for years as the wife of another laborer. After his promotion, Billy had wasted no time in his new position handing out jobs to friends and relatives, especially when he believed that they would "owe him one." Moira may have been used to the idea that she never knew what favors Billy was trying to curry, but this was a new one. A call from a female flunky at his job when that's where he was supposed to be? No wonder her sixth sense was tingling.

"That's just it, Moira. They found his MTD…" her voice drifted off. If Moira was vaguely annoyed at the call, the use of jargon irritated her even more. MTD? Motorized transportation device? Seriously? Moira knew the jargon and wasn't impressed.

"What do you mean they found his car? Where is HE?," she asked, raising an eyebrow.(Though this gesture was intimidating and even threatening when employed with her children, it was not particularly effective over the phone.)

"That's just it, we don't know…" she stammered. "We were hoping, that is, we thought maybe he went home."

For a moment, Moira too imagined Billy's funeral, albeit without bagpipes. She also contemplated the delightful stretch of years without needing to manage him, or his crazy schemes, of time alone with her children and choices made for herself. Just as quickly, she felt remorse for her callousness, and resolved to wait patiently for further news.

Hours went by as Moira waited for news. Another Sanitation Inspector stopped by to ask her questions. The Union called to tell her not to talk to anyone. Then finally, a call from the hospital. Billy was there, mostly all right, waiting to be released. He was calling form the ER, he said. He had fallen into a garbage truck he said but he wasn't badly hurt. Don't talk to anyone, he urged.

Billy's descent into the depths of the garbage maw and his resurrection against all odds several hours later created a crisis for many of those concerned.

Billy was a loyal and longstanding member of the NYC Sanitation Workers Union, founded in the tradition of labor unions to protect its workers from obvious safety issues, as well as promote collective bargaining. It was one of the largest of the NYC unions, and a member of the labor council of unions. In this instance, though, there was a collision of interests. The shop steward, John Moran, didn't like Billy, who he thought of as a nitwit, and he didn't like the way he acted since becoming an Inspector, handing out favors and ruling the roost in a way that he described to his wife as "like a little Napoleon." (John thought this line was particularly clever, and a tribute to all those hours he had spent reading Classics Illustrated comics. His wife gave her bored assent when he offered that self-assessment.) Worse, he was worried what Skeeter would think of any favoritism to Billy. John liked to lift a few at the Tamaqua with Skeeter, and he was a little afraid of him. Billy had already upset things by offering his wife Doozy a job, not only for the extra money but also so Doozy could keep an eye on John.

Then there was the head of the entire local, a cupcake named Alora Banquet, rumored to be a mistress of the Mayor himself. Alora immediately realized that the situation was touchy. On one hand, the rank and file viewed her with suspicion because she wasn't one of theirs. There were few women pulling trash to start with, and her giddy natural disposition didn't fit well with the Union's effort to find its place among the other biggies with the motto "NY's Strongest." On the other hand, failing to stand up for a union member injured, perhaps permanently, in a freak accident that smelled of safety breach didn't look good.

And then there was the Mayor himself, Hizzoner Horton Jackson Lee, whose innovative approach to increasing citations against lazy crews led to this problem. Lee's inner circle had been surprised by his announcement of his "Score for the Corps" program that allowed promotion points for writing citations against crews, since it was probably illegal under Civil Service rules. Even worse, it had been immediately re-labeled "Scores for Whores" by the rank and file. And there was the optics of a blood stained and uniformed City worker rising from the steaming trash heap of Great Kills, which community activists were scrambling to close. It was a public relations nightmare that desperately needed to disappear into the resounding silence of obscurity.

Luckily for everyone concerned, including Billy himself, in the end it was a small-time lawyer with the injury firm of Fisto, Kleinwold and Bing who happened to reach him first. Stephen Desomkowitzi happened to be in the emergency room of the hospital for a slip and fall case when he overhead two nurses talking about Billy and the accident. Excusing himself from his elderly patient, he sprinted down the hall to the greener pastures of Billy's bedside and the potential injury windfall of a big city case.

We should probably take a moment here to understand Billy's state of mind: when he had awakened inside the truck, he quickly cycled through a range of thoughts. After wondering where he was, he began to wonder where he would end up. Truthfully, as Billy's children could attest, the idea of an outlandish accident was not beyond the realm of his imagining. On almost a daily basis, Billy surveyed his surroundings for potential hazards, and day-dreamed about how he would escape should an accident befall him. He would, for example, point out a scruffily dressed traveler on the subway and nudge the child next to him, "what would you do if he leaped up to attack you with the ballpoint pen in his pocket?" (answer: gouge out his eyes.) The point of this dialogue of disaster was never the actual answer though. Billy didn't really feel fear himself, at least not in the conventional way. Rather, he was studying the child in question for a reaction, observing in detail the anxiety this might elicit, almost as if it energized him in some way.

Inside the truck Billy had assessed his situation, noted with interest that he might die and moved onto other thoughts rapidly. Much more disturbing to him was the feeling of emptiness, both the absence of others to respond to him and his inability to provoke fear or pity in others. When he was unceremoniously dumped out on a trash pile, his reaction was not so much joy at escaping death as a tick of recognition that there was an opportunity here to be exploited.

Like many Irishmen of his generation, Billy liked to invoke the spirit of President John F. Kennedy, especially an idea that he had once heard in a speech. The word crisis in Chinese, Kennedy said, is a combination of the characters for danger and opportunity. It was an idea that Billy would cling to with the tenaciousness of the half-educated despite many later public comments that this was not correct. This crisis of safety for Billy was a golden opportunity as well.

As Billy lay on a gurney in Our Lady of Perpetual Blessings hospital in Staten Island, he was as open as the Lady herself to the ministrations of the out of breath Stephen Desomkowitizi and the retainer agreement he waived at Billy. He would use this crisis (opportunity?) to make sure that his life changed for the better. When his new buddy Stephen suggested that he call his wife to make sure she agreed, Billy waived him off, signing the agreement and smiling to himself at the idea that this idiot was now "his" lawyer.

Three days later "his" lawyer was handing Billy a hastily generated six-figure check along with the paperwork for a disability pension that would allow him to retire early, as long as he left the state as soon as possible. This was Mayor Lee's clever addition to the deal, solely designed to get Billy and his family out of sight of the press ASAP. The airline tickets to a nice three weeker in Texas, on the beach, donated by the Union President was a bonus.

Still later when the family gathered for a retirement farewell in the backyard of his house, Billy's nephew would present him with a die-cast model of a garbage truck, painted with glittering gold paint.

Part Two – Flour Bluffs

"Many spiritual traditions recognize that when the 'dark one' appears [s]he is most beautiful, most wonderful and most engaging. The truth only comes out later..."
unknown

For the next three weeks, Billy and Moira and the two younger kids vacationed in Texas. Prior to this, family vacations were at best a road trip in their Volkswagen bus, camping in a huge army surplus canvas tent and eating cold sandwiches made from their battered blue Igloo cooler. During these trips resentment filled the air – for the parents that their sacrifice was not appreciated enough, and for the children that they felt confined to the small space of the bus and the company of their parents. Now the time and space to explore, the hotel accommodations (paid for by the Union!) and the anticipation of change created a holiday atmosphere that brought out their best.

Billy had spent most of his adult life finding ways to do the minimum possible at his job, and to get what he could from it. Friday nights usually included him arriving home with a duffle bag of acquisitions from the lost and found at the depot – forgotten clothing, sunglasses, and toys. Occasionally, he would arrive with a larger item of swag gleaned from the trash – a piece of furniture, or once a Nuc-hockey game. There was also a steady stream of household staples – small bars of soap, toilet paper, and even bread and fruit meant for the animals that he had stolen from his part-time job as a zookeeper (he drew the line at the meat intended for the lions; that was too disgusting.)

His older children had grown to be embarrassed by this petty theft and his insistence that they be complicitly appreciative of it. When Siobhan longed for the Wonder Bread she had seen on TV commercials, she was at first delighted with the giant waxed paper loaf that he brought home. It was only as she made a peanut butter sandwich that she noticed that the wrapper had no logo on it.

"Papa, why is the label blank?" She asked, her mind working as she chewed.

"Forget about it…" he answered

"This is from the gorillas, isn't it?" she screamed, spitting out the food and running away.

His answer, "what the hell's the matter with you?" was his standard reply, transforming his embarrassing daily thefts into an incidence of the children's ingratitude. Worse, he often brought home items that were useless to his family but that he couldn't resist taking – goalie pads (none of his children skated) or clothing that didn't fit anyone. Moira would shake her head and ask, "why did you even bring this home?" Angry, he would clarify, "they didn't need it."

On the Texas trip there was little of this, though their suitcase had begun to be filled with tiny bars of soap and miniature bottles of shampoo that they might need later. More significantly, Billy had begun to change his orientation from what he needed to get next, to what he was going to do without the day-to-day structure of work.

By the end of their three weeks, they had arrived in the Gulf coast town of Corpus Christi without finding the place where they wanted to land permanently, and it was here that the real transformation began. Corpus Christi was a smaller town than they were used to as native New Yorkers, but it had the sunshine and the water that they associated with the good life. Moira was immediately taken by the birds that sought refuge in the twin islands, Padre and Mustang, that sheltered the bay. There were birds everywhere – sea birds that were familiar, and pink tinged birds with long spoon shaped bills, pelicans with basket shaped beaks, and song birds unseen but trilling loudly from the trees. Billy liked the canals that wound their way through the residential areas, emptying in the Gulf of Mexico. Here he could have a large sailboat and perhaps entice Liam, his oldest son, to help him captain it.

But it was the city tour they booked, an hour-long excursion on a rickety converted school bus painted over with palm trees, that really sold Billy. The guide had told the story of a particular neighborhood, Flour Bluffs, that had gotten its name during the early 19th century Pastry Wars (an episode not covered in most of them Yankee school books.) Rebellious Mexicans had fought a turf war that prevented the local French pastry chefs from importing flour. In frustration, Mexican smugglers had dumped barrels of flour in the area. To Billy the idea of defiantly dumping flour assumed the grandeur of the Boston tea party.

The next day he drove around Flour Bluffs until he located the enclave he wanted: Cabeza de Vaca Estates, situated on a canal system and surrounded by a stuccoed stone wall. Billy didn't know and wouldn't have cared that the development had been the work of a low-level Mafia thug named Tony "the Eel" Pelligrino, who had been exiled from the more convivial confines of Miami when he joined the witness protection program. He didn't understand what Cabeza de Vaca meant, or even that he had been a Spanish explorer. Billy didn't need to know any of that. All he knew was that he liked the look of the canals; he liked the classy Manatee club inside even more, with its plantation style colonnade. Best of all, he liked the house for sale he saw on a corner lot, with a dock and a little gazebo. And he liked that Moira charmed the elderly owner over tea, talking him into taking the For Sale sign off the lawn without even a deposit. They signed the papers before they returned to New York to pack.

By the time that Billy and Moira moved to Flour Bluffs, their three older children were young adults. The gap in ages was by no means unusual among the large Irish families that surrounded them, but Moira explained the phenomena by saying she felt like they had two families. Partially this was because of the distance that would separate them, but this feeling also arose because that there had been a change in the culture of the family as the relationships shifted among them.

The older children, each in their own way, had loved growing up near the water in Gerritsen Beach, acquiring an independence of spirit as they navigated their interests. Charlie (short for Siobhan) loved the small-town atmosphere of the isolated enclave. Liam, the oldest son, who insisted on "Liam" because he couldn't stand that he was named for his father, loved the water and sailing. Monica, the youngest of the first family, also loved the water, and followed in Liam' footsteps devotedly. We will learn more about them all later, but for now, we will turn our attention to the third daughter, Luna Lynn Quinn.

If Billy and his choices was the center of the first part of our story, Luna Lynn Quinn, his youngest daughter and truest heir, will be the center of all that follows. Billy had chosen Luna's name, a fanciful branding of this daughter that he understood was more decidedly his than the others, a creature metaphorically, if not actually, of the emptiness of night. She was a true heir to his internal emptiness, his need to fill it with nothing that could ever satisfy – not possessions, not relationships, and especially not emotion. Where Billy may have been parasitical in his relationship to the world, Luna was all predator.

Worse, when the move to Texas was complete, Billy was free to obsessively devote his free time to Luna, laying away collateral, he was sure, for the daughter who would lavish him with devotion later. It was a pit into which the whole family began to slowly sink, a void that could never be filled. Luna surveyed her surroundings and continually resented the ways in which she didn't fit, beginning with those closest to her and spiraling outwards. She had also absorbed a lifetime worth of manipulation techniques.

To be sure, Cabeza de Vaca estates was not a place that had attracted young families with children. The small lots and canals were designed with retirees in mind, a place to fulfill the dream of having a boat and the reality of gathering at the local Manatee Club to socialize while it sat unused at the dock. The larger neighborhood of Flour Bluffs, where Luna and her younger brother Omar Bradley went to school, on the other hand, was affluent to an extent that evoked envy from Luna. She didn't fit easily into the social context of the other girls. Her Brooklyn accent, her clothes that came from Sears, and her older parents all made her an outlier from the start. Nor did she get the get the jokes or understand the emotions that the others seemed to feel, though she did her best to laugh or mimic what she saw, if only a bit behind.

Through high school she followed the social cues that she saw around her, joining Dance Line, keeping pace academically in a mediocre, disinterested way, cycling through friends and male companions if they were interesting or useful. Her peers paid lip service to her friendship, viewing her with a wariness that she recognized not as hurtful but only as vaguely annoying. For several years she amused herself with tormenting Omar Bradley by using him as camouflage: whenever he found a group of friends or an activity that mattered to him, she was not far behind, even trying out the junior ROTC club when he did, though she complained bitterly that the rifles were heavy, in drab colors and the boys were nerdy. It wasn't long before he caught on to this scheme. Billy wouldn't hear that Luna was at fault in any way. "What the hell's the matter with you?" he shouted at Omar Bradley, "she's your SISTER," as if that explained all. Later Omar Bradley would understand that this standard response was a suggestion that boundaries shouldn't matter where your family was concerned. Moira understood that Omar Bradley needed his own space, and that Luna's motives were not pure. In fact, she knew that Luna only joined these groups for a way into emotion or belonging. It ultimately didn't even matter if she was accepted, because she didn't feel anything either way: it was only an opportunity to ruin it for him, or to make herself a victim.

It was at a cross-country track club meet that Omar Bradley finally reached his breaking point. He was surprisingly fast and loved the peace of the longer runs, often through the woods instead of around an oval. In the morning heats, Omar Bradley had placed first, his time on track to set a state record. Luna, on the other hand, had disgraced herself, first finishing dead last in a long run and then deliberately tripping a teammate that she found annoying in the relay. The Coach had witnessed the incident, and, not believing Luna's tearful apology, had banned her from the afternoon finals.

Luna went straight to Moira and sobbingly proclaimed the whole track club lame. Moira was not moved, finding her seat on the bleachers to watch Omar Bradley run the finals. Luna wouldn't take no for an answer, and finding a pay phone, called Billy with a sobbing appeal to pick her up. Billy was doubly annoyed: he didn't like that his afternoon of peace was being interrupted. This was not fun for him. He also didn't like that Moira was selfishly ignoring Luna for that Omar Bradley, who was not fun at all. Before the afternoon session had even started, he was at the track, chewing out the Coach, fetching Moira from the stands by snapping his fingers and telling Omar Bradley that he was finished with track. The perplexed Coach took Moira aside (as the only sane one between the two of them) and urged her to reconsider. "He has a chance," he pleaded, "to make it to the state finals." Shaking her head, Moira said that it was the pair of them – Luna and Omar Bradley – or neither one. She couldn't afford the weeks of recriminations, arguments and passive aggressive slights from both Luna and Billy. It was relentless and exhausting. Omar Bradley would understand.

Except that he didn't. The incident was a turning point for him. Realizing that the only way out was escape, he first retreated into himself, leaving his bedroom only to go to school and then retreating back inside. Weeks later the track coach took him aside. Think about getting out, he counseled, before you end up like some of the others. Omar Bradley, always sensitive to language wasn't sure if the reference to "the others" meant his family or the others in town. In any case, the next day Omar Bradley saw the local Air Force recruiter, opting to finish high school early. Within six months, he was headed to South Korea and a stint with the missile command. With no one left at home to manipulate or torture, and with her future prospects dwindling, Luna decided to cement her Southern Belle bona fides by applying to the University of Mississippi, or "Ole Miss," largely because some of her classmates described it as "hardcore southern."

It may have seemed an unlikely choice for Luna to gravitate to an old Southern university like Ole Miss. She was after all, originally a Brooklyn girl, transplanted to Texas, but not genuinely a native of either. Fundamentally, Luna didn't really feel at home anywhere, or perhaps it would be more accurate to say that she didn't feel anything at all anyway. If any place could have felt like home to Luna, Ole Miss seemed like a natural fit. Over the years it had been the center of any number of controversial racist incidents, from resisting integration to fraternity brothers posing provocatively near Emmett Till's grave. The air fairly crackled with the tension, anguish, and the drama of fraught feelings. It was an elixir to Luna's soul. From the beginning she embraced all the gestures of an Ole Miss Rebel, from the shouted greeting "Hotty Totty" to the deep southern drawl. And then there were the sororities.

Ole Miss had participated in Greek Life from early in its history. Kappa Sigma Mu was one of the oldest of the sororities, housed in a lovely faux plantation style house on sorority row. Luna had carefully researched the sorority offerings, ultimately deciding that Kappa was the one for her. The sisters seemed the most stylish, the loudest and the most confident of any of the sororities on campus. Every gathering sizzled with the electricity of an unfolding performance. Every encounter was a carefully veiled pit fight among vipers. It was truly, wonderfully delicious. The only problem was that she was not included on the Kappa rush list. For one thing, she was a "Yankee;" for another, she didn't have the graceful manners, the "butter wouldn't melt in her mouth" charm of a Kappa. She also didn't have any of the trappings of a Southern belle: the expensive car, taste in clothing, or sense of style.

Ultimately, Luna's fate on the rush list was decided as the result of a power struggle between two senior Kappas, neither of whom wanted Luna, but each of whom was determined not to let the other win. A small act of sabotage by each resulted in two fewer candidates for rush, and a scramble to find at least one replacement. That's where Luna came in. During Rush Week, or Kappa Katapult as it was called, Luna enthusiastically embraced every bit of hazing thrown her way, tearfully accepting the many punishments inflicted on her until the sisters couldn't help but accept her out of plain guilt. Later, when Luna was a senior Kappa, the sisters would cringe at the cruelty that she would gleefully inflict on her own rushes.

As a Kappa sister, Luna shined. She was charming to every other sister who ranked in the hierarchy, and insidiously, covertly cruel to those who didn't. It wasn't long before she gained a reputation as game for anything, with a ready vocabulary of sly barbs ready to wound those who dared to aspire above their station. The victims of her ugly side were never really sure what had happened and could never point to anything that she had done overtly that was unambiguously unkind. As Mary Beth Hollander, the alpha Kappa said, "that Luna is just so fun…"

Academically, Luna didn't fare as well. It was hard to keep track of those annoying assignments when she had so many important social obligations. She had started with the idea that she would be pre-med. She liked the idea of how she would look in a white coat and enjoyed the fantasy of having the lives of vulnerable people hang in the balance. It wasn't long before she abandoned that idea; a semester of volunteering at the hospital cemented her change of heart. You might think the inspiration to serve as a volunteer was a requirement of the pre-med degree, or you may suspect a burst of altruism from Luna, but you would be wrong. Truthfully, tequila was the prime mover in this experience.

Searching for better MRS hunting grounds, Luna had tried to enter a new student club. Already locked and loaded with several shots of tequila (her drink of choice largely because it was cheap, and was readily disguisable in Mountain Dew), she presented a fake ID at the door. The bouncer was not distracted by Luna's signature flirting, and easily spotted the fake ID. When her next level flirting didn't smooth her entrance, she became enraged and threw her cup at him, adding a racial slur as she walked away. Unfortunately, he had turned out to be the son of the Dean. Without remorse, she looked at her community service disciplinary sentence as an opportunity to pad her resume and embraced the first few weeks with enthusiasm. Quickly learning that none of the staff was interested in her opinion, that she couldn't wear a white coat, and that illness was often messy and fraught with little gratitude to volunteers, she began to question her career ambitions. A failing grade in remedial math sealed the deal, and led to her transfer to an Education major.

Luna didn't really like children. They were loud, messy, needy, and a lot of work. Her sorority sister, Mary Beth, soon helped her see past those obstacles towards her new goal. "First," she said, ticking off on a finely manicured finger, "the major is easy – all finger puppets and cheerful signs. Second, you would get every summer off to work on your tan. Most important though," she said with careful emphasis, "you don't really want a job or a degree. Girl, you're here for the MRS degree, and the guys all want an Ed major. They think it means you're already committed to children, and therefore sex, and they think you can help them with homework."

Luna embraced her new calling with a passion, though truthfully, she didn't fare much better than she had in pre-med. Her instructors were often perplexed about her lack of the most basic knowledge ("there are 13 stripes on an American flag, Luna, for the 13 colonies.") and concerned about her apparent disdain for children. Using a loophole, she did her student teaching in Ireland, believing that it would be easy to finish the assignment and pub-crawl in the evenings. Besides, those little blonde-haired kids would be so grateful to her. She was assigned to Sister Mary Immaculata Murphy at Saint Brigid's Academy in Dublin.

Sister Mary was a formidable presence in the school, having been a teacher for well over 50 years. Most of the parish or their parents had Sr. Mary at one point or another in their elementary career. As she grew older, the decision was taken to put her in charge of supervising the study abroad students, most of whom were on just this side of finding another career. Sr. Mary's mission was to mold them into shape with a combination of tough love, stern looks and positive reinforcement. Later she would describe Luna as her biggest failure – a student teacher who made her deeply uneasy. When the Mother Superior reviewed Luna's grade, an "unsatisfactory," she was forced to remind Sr. Mary that St. Bride's "really can't do without the income from the Americans, even when they're a loopy lot." Reluctantly, Sr. Mary changed her assessment to "satisfactory", mollifying her unease with an evaluation that stated in part, "…working with Luna as a student teacher mentee was a truly memorable experience. Luna Quinn is a genuine standout in my fifty years of supervision. Her skills are adequate; her smile is pleasant, and I am especially pleased to note that she intends to return to her home country to pursue her intended career."

Several months later, Luna finished her degree   a Bachelor of Science, she was careful to note, in Education. Masking her disappointment in not earning her MRS like that nasty Mary Beth, Luna returned home to Corpus Christi ready to find a job.

Luna may have been disappointed by her return to Flour Bluffs, but Billy picked up where he had left off, bragging lavishly about his daughter who went to Ole Miss. (By now, Monica had earned a PhD at from Cornell as an aerospace engineer, and Omar Bradley had been accepted early to Harvard Law School. Billy hardly noticed.) When a stranger at the Manatee Club patiently explained to him that these later two accomplishments were distinctively more prestigious, he eyed him suspiciously, vowing inwardly to never return there except for Tuesday Chicken Wing night. At home he would tell Moira, "Anyone who is against Luna is against me", a phrase that he would repeat frequently over the next several years.

By the fall, she had settled into a job at a local elementary school in a supplementary modular building in the far less affluent neighborhood of North Bluffs. Her daily round of tending to the needs of her class of second graders and returning home to Billy and Moira in her used diesel Rabbit made her burn with a slow fury. Determined to change her life, she began dating with a new interest, and it wasn't long before a likely candidate waltzed into her life.

She met Dimitris Spankendopoulos at a dinner for Ole Miss alums held at the Manatee Club. Moira, who had become very active in the club, working as a bartender, and serving as Floating Secretary (the equivalent of a President in the nautically themed hierarchy), had arranged the evening hoping to end some of Luna's bitter carping. Dimitris, known as Jimmy to his friends, was not an Ole Miss alum. He had been hired for the evening to serve as a kind of host, largely because he had a particularly flashy blue suit.

Luna arrived drunk, having primed herself to meet someone with several large water glasses of tequila as she was dressing. When Jimmy came over to her immediately, shepherding her to a table in the corner, she naturally assumed it was because he was so drawn to personal magnetism. When he continued to bring her drinks, and even plates of chicken wings, she knew she had landed a good one. Moira noticed how far-gone Luna was from across the room and to stave off disaster had told Jimmy that he should sit with her and then quietly escort her home. When Jimmy sat down at the small table, Luna knew she had him hooked.

Surveying his dark Mediterranean eyes, curly brown hair and olive skin, she listened in studied fascination as he explained that he was an entrepreneur (he owned a flatbed truck that he used to deliver Porta-potties for *Johnny Come Lately*) and that though he had inherited some of his wealth (a collection of Hummel figures, $1,000 in Savings Bonds and a Bicentennial plate left him by his single mother), his photogenic memory had helped him earn all the rest. It wasn't many minutes later before Luna left with Jimmy. The inevitable followed. Later still, before the wedding reception at the Manatee for their shotgun marriage, Jimmy would tell Moira that when he saw Luna, he knew he had to have her. Maybe it was her Ruebenesque nose. He just knew that a rolling stone gathers no moths.

Part Three – Becoming the Black Sheep

"Exile is like death. You cannot understand it until it happens to you." Golshifteh Farahani

Greek mythology tells the story of a beautiful woman named Cassandra, daughter of King Priam of Troy. It seems that she had been spotted by the god Apollo, who was immediately overcome with love for her. Desiring her, he offered the gift of prophecy on the condition she would be his lover. Cassandra accepted the gift, but then refused to allow Apollo into her bed, angering him and causing him to curse her: from then on, Cassandra would have the gift of sight, but no one would believe her visions.

Monica, the middle of Billy's family and an aficionado of Greek mythology, often thought of this story. In one way or another, all the others – Siobhan, Liam, Monica and even Omar Bradley - each could see the ways in which first Billy, and then Luna, was corrupting the family and trying to manipulate each of them in turn. Still, as their vision unfolded, the price they paid was that the others couldn't believe the truth of what was happening. It may have been a gift to see, to have the scales lifted from their eyes, but like Cassandra, no one believed.

With the move to Corpus Christi, the emotional constellation of the family was re-defined. Siobhan, Liam and Monica had not made the move south, each for their own reasons. The distance, coupled with the effect of many manipulations and outright lies, first from Billy, and then from Luna, shifted these three firmly to the periphery of family significance. The process was a gradual erosion, largely unrecognizable to each victim as it was occurring, with a creeping process of family gossip, lies and petty exclusions. Omar Bradley would also join this circle, which he dubbed "the Others."

Siobhan, who didn't recognize her status among the Others until the last, was most confused and hurt by the change. She was certain that all would be made right if only she could reason with her parents; but Omar Bradley and the rest realized this was futile. As Omar Bradley began to practice law, he explained what would happen in terms that he understood as a version of the "four dog defense."

"Imagine that you are defending the owner of a dog who has just bitten someone," he said. "You start by saying 'that's not my dog.' If the plaintiff proves it is your dog, you move to defense number two, denial – 'if it is my dog, it didn't bite you.' Then, if they can prove a bite, you argue defense number three, denial of the injury – 'it may have bitten you, but it didn't actually hurt you.' Finally, if they prove injury, you move to your final dog defense, distraction – 'what did you do to provoke my dog?'"

Over the years, whenever Luna had committed some outrage, Billy would angrily move through a version of this litany, Omar Bradley pointed out. Mimicking Billy's characteristic angry whine, he ticked them off on his hand:

> "1) she's your sister! (*implication, it's us against the world and even if she did it, you shouldn't tell anyone*), 2) she didn't really do that! (*And by the way, what the hell's the matter with you that you would think that?*) 3) she didn't mean it! (*Again, what is wrong with you that you believe she would be so mean?!*) and finally, 4) what did you do to her?"

It was a disturbing form of rationalization that always left the Others questioning their own judgment, motivations, and even reality. It was no surprise in some ways that when Billy and Moira moved to Texas, the Others didn't follow. With the distance came a gradual understanding that the family they had grown up with was not what it had always seemed.

To the outside world, Billy was a great provider, a rags-to-riches story of his own. Raised in an orphanage, he found his way to owning a store, then a solidly working-class civil service job with a respectably sunny retirement. Along the way, he married a beautiful, intelligent, hard-working woman and he raised five kids who found stable relationships, college, careers, and families of their own. What more could anyone ask for? In the early years, Billy was fond of pointing out to Moira that "at least" he didn't drink away his paycheck or beat her. ("A low bar," as she often thought.)

At the same time, the children of Billy's "first family" – Siobhan, Liam, and Monica - gradually understood that this was not the complete truth. Thinking back, Monica realized that while Billy had provided many things, they were often not quite right. Everything he gave them in fact, was in fact an approximation of a need, served up to silence them into complicit gratitude. When they longed for Wonder Bread, he brought them bread stolen during his part time job at the zoo. When Siobhan longed for a Barbie, he brought her a Beautiful Betty that he found on the cheap at John's Bargain stores, insisting that she accept the compromise gift with lavish appreciation, embracing lower expectations – she only "needed" a knockoff doll. On a regular basis he committed petty theft, or liberated things from the Lost and Found, all of it wrapped in a cloak of complicit gratitude. It was not only a parade of near misses, it also required immediate praise, or they risked having the gift removed suddenly, and with stealth. Nothing was ever really "yours," Monica thought later, it remained "his." And if he perceived that you didn't need it anymore, he could take it abruptly away.

For Billy, it was convenience coupled with true power. As swiftly as he could fulfill a need with something they didn't even want, he could take it away, all the while denying that they ever had it. Ingratitude was a suggestion that they didn't need it, or a justification for the theft since others didn't need it. Billy was the arbiter of what they had, what they deserved, and they should all be grateful. To the Others, nothing ever felt secure.

When Billy and Moira moved to Texas, it was in some ways natural that the three oldest children wouldn't follow. By now, they had careers and families of their own, and it was unreasonable to expect them to uproot themselves to follow. Still, Billy was annoyed that most of his source of entertainment was gone. Worse, Moira seemed to think it was okay to neglect him now that he needed her most.

Through most of their married life, Moira had worked at a series of part time jobs, balancing them with her care for the children and their friends. It hadn't been long before neighboring mothers discovered that Moira was always willing to feed a child or keep them entertained. It was an easy out for them to let their kids play with the Quinn children while they took time for themselves. Billy preferred the company of the guys at work, often staying out late and then disappearing early in the morning. He seemed unconcerned about anything that happened at home unless it had the potential for being fun for him. It was important for Monica to have violin lessons because he could envision himself listening to "gypsy violins" in a romantic movie. It was important for Siobhan to get an LPN certificate from community college so someone would massage his feet when he got older. And it was important for Liam to learn small engine repair, so Billy would have someone to fix his outboards and lawn mowers. None of these things had worked out the way Billy wanted. Even Moira was drifting away.

Moira at first bristled at retirement. Even with two younger children at home, Billy's demands for the center place in her attention continued. Soon, she learned that the Others were a source of escape – though they all led busy, successful lives and they were only too happy to have Moira visit them and the growing group of grandchildren. Luna needed something to return herself to the limelight; to refocus Moira and Billy's attention where it belonged. Later the Others would recognize that it was all a process, and they would remember Omar Bradley's "Four Dog

Defense." Monica's wife, Belle Notte, described it differently: as the "Four Stages of Shunning."

First, Luna would create a situation designed to make her appear to be a victim, Bella Notte said. This was easily accomplished by pressing all the right buttons, but only when were no witnesses. Next, there was a response, Luna would make sure it came in public, with the maximum amount of anger and a suitably tearful response from Luna. Then came a round of family gossip, where the story took its natural course among the spouses, cousins, and grandchildren, escalating until it had reached its own natural critical mass. Finally, there was a session of cementing alliances among all the constituencies. Usually this also involved an "accidental" mention of a family secret orchestrated to elevate tension. If all else failed, there were always invitations that went astray or a session of whispering in Billy's ear.

Each of the three older Others were independent in their own way. They had been left behind physically with the move to Texas; they had their own families, careers and soon they became Moira's refuge. They each believed in the idea of family unity; that they could trust each other at least against the world. As might be expected, each in turn grew into an identity that was distinct from their original family in surprising ways. These were all reasons to annoy Billy and Luna. So, one-by-one they were pushed aside.

By the time of the garbage truck and the move, Siobhan had been married for several years. Her early marriage to a neighborhood friend of Liam's from high school seemed the logical and right step for this stage of her life. Most of her friends married early or worked in the civil service.

Her husband, Michael Flaherty, had graduated with an electrical engineering degree from Brooklyn Tech at a time when computers were new. Mike used his entry-level job at a large bank to work hard and climb the career ladder, rising rapidly through the ranks to a directorship position. His quiet intelligence and natural inquisitiveness made him an easy choice when there was a complicated assignment to complete.

Siobhan settled into her Connecticut home equally easily, raising the three active sons who came in quick succession. She filled her time with all the activities of a busy suburban housewife but retained her mother's intellectual curiosity: she read avidly, joined social groups, learned about languages, cultures, and history. Her large house and successful children would become the first focus of Luna's envy. Eyeing Siobhan's preppy style of dressing, Luna would say that she was, "a mannish dresser who got her sense of fashion from her son's hand-me-downs." It would have been natural at this point for Siobhan to attend college, but after trying a few courses she decided it wasn't really for her. The courses were narrowly focused on career goals, not inviting any exploration, and worse they took time away from her family.

Once a month, she attended a book club meeting, with books chosen by the members from a vast list of history, philosophy, and literature. The club members took turns hosting the meetings and providing each other with handouts of background for each book. Siobhan loved these discussions, carefully reading and filling her books with post-it notes marking interesting passages and important questions. When Moira visited, Siobhan took her as a guest to a meeting, irritating Luna at a distance when she heard about it. "I don't have time for book clubs," she remarked disdainfully, "especially since they're just an excuse to stick a straw in a bottle of Chardonnay."

It was shortly after this trip that Siobhan joined a gym, arriving early every morning after dropping her boys off at school. At first Siobhan used various pieces of equipment to exercise: the treadmill, a stair-stepper, or a bicycle. Soon bored, she decided to try a Tai Chi class early one morning. Watching through the glass back wall, she saw an older Asian woman with a taut body and silver hair leading a group of women through what looked like a graceful dance of hand movements and slow poses. She slipped inside, joining the back row. Before this class she had been too intimidated to join any of the other exercise classes. They seemed to be filled with energetic young women who knew the workout routines and the inside jokes from the instructors. More than that, these women saw themselves as athletes, or at least as housewife-athletes. Siobhan didn't know if she saw herself that way, any more than she saw herself as a college student or even exclusively a housewife, but she loved the challenge of remembering the movements; of keeping time with the rest of the class.

In the evenings, she began to read books that were not on her book club list: books about Asian philosophy, history and culture. The *Analects of Confucius* made her think about what a family meant, while books of ancient Chinese history introduced her to a culture that had evolved through thousands of years of isolation. She carried a thick paperback copy of *The Dream of the Red Chamber*, with her for weeks, diving into the complex relationships of the many characters as she waited to pick up her sons from after school activities. She took a class at the community college on speaking Mandarin and discovered that she had an ability to speak that surprised her. When Mike was out of town, she traveled to the New York city to explore Chinatown, at first alone and later as a regular adventure with Monica. It was a full-scale immersion, almost a secret world that she carried with her everywhere she went.

One morning their Tai Chi teacher, Ellen announced that they would try an exercise called, *tuishou* or "Push Hands."

"It's too easy," Ellen said, her feet spread wide, "to think of Tai Chi as a 'lady game'. No!" she continued, loudly. "Tai Chi is a marital art. We may not practice punching, kicking and beating people with sticks…that's too easy! No, we use the *ba men*, the 'eight gates' to find leverage, balance and delicate timing of movements!"

The class looked at each other. It sounded impossible. Siobhan thought briefly of using this moment of hesitancy to slip out the door. This sounded too much, too confrontational. Looking up though, she realized that Ellen was looking directly at her.

"All of you think," Ellen continued, "that the way to counter force is with force. Wrong! What happens," she asked, rhetorically, "when two cars head towards each other at fifty miles per hour? Bang!" she said, explosively, stamping her foot on the floor.

Siobhan was listening, fascinated. "It's a no brainer. Resist force by waiting for the right moment and redirecting it. Siobhan, come up here."

Siobhan reddened. She had never been singled out like this, but she had missed her moment to slip away. Ellen positioned herself in front of Siobhan, her slightly longer torso intimidating up close. "Stand so," Ellen continued, placing their right hands back-to-back and their left hands against each other's forearms. Speaking in a low voice to Siobhan, she said, "empty your mind, and when the moment is right, try and push me over."

Siobhan focused on the energy she could feel at the light touch of Ellen's hands. The muscles felt coiled, like a spring waiting to explode into action. Counting mentally, Siobhan drove forward towards Ellen. In one swift motion, Ellen guided her to the floor.

"It's all about feeling the intent," Ellen said, standing over Siobhan, "and feeling your connection to the earth. Remember that you don't have to resist energy or redirect it to gain an advantage. It's all about *ting jing*, listening power."

Ellen helped Siobhan up, then paired her with a much taller and younger partner. Tentatively, they lined themselves up as Ellen had directed. Usually impatient, Siobhan found peace in the long, silent waiting for her partner to move. In the moments of anticipation, she could sense her partner's gathering motivation, waiting patiently to step slightly to the side as her partner lunged forward, ending up on the ground. Smiling inwardly, Siobhan felt that she had arrived emotionally at a place that made sense. Here was an activity that she could master: an identity that clicked. By the end of the class, she had defeated each opponent.

Over the course of the next weeks, Siobhan was invited to a local *tai chi* center, where she further developed her push hands skills. Within a few months, she entered a local tournament, returning home with an enormous trophy to the amusement of her sons. Push Hands was soon a part of her regular routine, and by the end of that first year, she had her first national ranking. It had become as much a center of who Siobhan was as her life within her own family. Her only wish was that she could use it when it came to the Quinns.

The Texas family believed that they continued to be an important part of Siobhan's life. The truth was far more complicated. Siobhan and her family were often the center of larger family events in their Connecticut home, mostly when the Texans wanted an excuse to visit the Northeast. Often, Siobhan was left wondering how much she really could trust them. Repeatedly too, she was left surprised to discover all the ways that surface appearance was a distortion of an ugly reality: that many lies were being told. Still, Siobhan was genuinely optimistic, pushing aside her doubts until the next incident. She would be the last one to realize the truth.

From a young age, Liam loved the blank spaces at the edges of the old maps in his history books. The text itself was difficult to understand, a jumble of meaningless shapes that blurred and collided, fading off to nothing at the end. Moira realized early on that there was something wrong with his vision. She wanted to take him to the specialist that the pediatrician recommended or get him fitted with special glasses. Billy was annoyed that everything revolved around Liam and his needs. Where was the money and the time for him? Moira tried to compromise, to keep the peace by taking him to the clinic, having him fitted with a version of the glasses that were big, cheap and clunky. Liam hated them. Hated the teasing, and it wasn't long before he claimed to have lost them somewhere. This only confirmed Billy's idea that it was all a big waste, a concession to "Madison Ave," which apparently dictated trends in medicine as well as hygiene. Soon, Liam had retreated to his bedroom, staring out his window at the lobster boats heading out through the canals to the Long Island Sound, and filling in the blank spaces in the maps in his mind.

One day, he passed through the garage on his way to the dock. As he did so, Billy was having a fit over a small outboard motor that he had bought that wasn't working. Billy had never really understood mechanical things, a fault he blamed on the nuns at the orphanage, as well as the string of foster fathers he had later. The truth was more complicated. While it was true that the nuns were only academically oriented, the foster fathers had tried to get Billy engaged in traditionally male things. Most of them were hard working laborers who had taken in children with their wives to help make ends meet, but also to pass something intangible on to the next generation. Billy was a difficult foster child to have. Some said sneaky, even given to petty thefts and small fires. Most of all, he didn't warm up to any gestures of affection. When

Billy's last foster father, a burly machinist named Logan Buckley, offered Billy the money to buy his first house, he took the money with a shrug. It was the least he could do, Billy thought. It was no surprise, then, that Billy had reached his breaking point with the small engine. What was the use, anyway? He only bought it because everyone else seemed to envy his house on the water and his boats. Angrily throwing a wrench across the garage, he spotted Liam.

"Can I try, Dad?" Liam asked, tentatively eyeing the engine that seemed a marvel of interlocking parts and gears. "You?" Billy snorted, viewing his son, "tell you what, if you can fix it, you can have it," he said, laughing to himself in the certainty that the challenge would keep him busy and frustrated for hours to come. Several hours later the growl of a small engine brought him running to the dock. There was Liam, the small engine mounted on the transom of a small rowboat roaring out towards the bay.

Later Liam would explain quietly to Moira that it all just made sense to him. Taking an engine apart he could see how and why it all fit; sense where it went wrong. She encouraged his passion and independence by buying him tools and manuals. Neighbors saw that he was a natural mechanic and were soon bringing him small engines, lawn mowers, hedge trimmers, and boat engines to repair. Saturdays often saw a line outside the Quinn garage of customers for his repair services. Soon, he had bought himself his first sailboat with the repair money, and he began teaching himself navigation and cabinet making. When it came time for high school, Moira signed a permission slip for him to take the test for specialty school, delighting when he got in. Billy dismissed the placement as a mistake, and then later convinced all who would listen that it was a glorified vocational high school.

High school really changed Liam. He grew tall and lean, his hair bleached blonde from his time in the sun working on boats. The curriculum was hard, but he was a master mechanic, an essential skill that no one else had. Soon he was trading his expert advice in shop classes for help in the more academic assignments. His new confidence affected his relationship with Billy as well. Determined to connect with him, Liam tried introducing him to some of the classical music records he had started to enjoy, an activity that Billy pronounced "boring."

Rebuffed, Liam retreated into his latest project, repairing a small boat, and gradually outfitting it with all the equipment he would need to entertain himself on the water – water skis, tow ropes and life jackets. The next step was to experiment with Monica and Siobhan driving the boat, so he could learn to ski. Finally, he was ready to invite high school friends for an adventure.

It wasn't long before every weekend included a rotating group of giddy city teenagers, who were delighted with the idea of waterskiing trips. Increasingly, these Saturday adventures attracted Billy's attention. His low-level annoyance that one of his kids was popular (*read: didn't need him*) and having fun that didn't include him, soon bloomed into full scale resentment. Billy tried to put a damper on it through a variety of unsuccessful manipulative parental edicts: you have to take your sisters (*sure – he liked their company*); you have to clean up the boat afterwards (*sure – Liam got the passengers to do it*); you have to eat breakfast first (*sure – Liam bought donuts when he was gassing the boat.*) Finally, at the end of his patience, Billy came up with a final demand.

"There's a safety concern," he insisted. "You're skiing around Mau Mau" (an island in the middle of the bay with hidden pilings from an aborted long forgotten bridge-building project.) "There could be a serious accident. Any serious accident would mean a hit to my homeowner's insurance," he said. (Liam noted that he wasn't concerned about any of the people involved, including his own son.) "You are forbidden to ski," Billy said empathically, grabbing the skis from the garage. "I can't even trust you," he continued, ignoring the irony of preaching trust, as well as the fact that all the skiing equipment belonged to Liam himself.

Liam was frustrated and furious, but also aware that all the cards in this situation lay in Billy's hands. It was a final childhood lesson in arbitrary power, manipulation, and passive-aggressive behavior. That night Liam went to the garage and removed a key ground wire from the engine, disabling it. When days later, Billy wanted to use the boat and couldn't start it, he went to find Liam. "Hey, I couldn't start the Johnson" he said, convinced that Liam had left it without gas. Liam barely glanced at him. "It's not working," he said, walking away.

Liam was surprised several weeks later when Billy woke him up early, eager to go with him on a "secret mission." "Don't tell anyone," Billy urged, "it's our secret." Together they put on bathing suits. Billy already had a jerry can and his new Super-8 movie camera waiting on the dock. Liam thought that they might be going out to the roamer shoals in his motorboat. When he headed to the boat though, Billy called him back. "No, no, I want you to swim across the canal with this can to the barge across the way. I left enough air in the can so it will float. I'm going to film it."

"What for?" Liam asked, confused.

"Pour the gas on the deck of the barge," Billy continued, "and go to the stern. Before you dive off, light these waterproof matches and throw them on that pile of rags at the back."

The barge was approximately 100 feet long with a flat bed and a wheelhouse amidships. It had once belonged to the nearby lobster fishery, but had it been sold some six months before, sitting at the dock awaiting renovations. "Irish Joe" Buchannan, a retired transit worker and sometime bartender at the Tamaqua bar lived on board, sleeping on a cot in the wheelhouse. Irish Joe had promised to fix up the barge and move it, but it had become increasingly clear that he was content to live right there on the canal. Billy was enraged at the eyesore in his view, as he soaked in his bathtub with the window overlooking the canal. The sight of it was a rebuke – a reminder that some people did whatever they wanted. By now, the Quinns had lived in the neighborhood for more than ten years. Each of the neighbors knew the children, and Moira, but none of them really knew Billy. He had nothing but disdain for them, telling his family that most of them were either "cat-lovers or bed-wetters." Billy was always happy to explain that cat-lovers might be bad because they had chosen to lavish attention on an animal, instead of an orphan child. Even Hitler loved dogs, he would continue. Bed-wetters were somehow worse, he reasoned. They lacked control: the worst sin in his book. In any case, Billy knew that he couldn't get neighbors to agree to help him. Liam would do, and he would film the whole thing. But now, it seemed that Liam was pushing back.

"Are you crazy?" Liam whispered, conscious of the early hour and the neighbors who might hear them. "Irish Joe might be asleep in the cabin...and someone might see me."

"What the hell's the matter with you?" Billy countered, his voice rising, "I'm your FATHER. No one's around, and Irish Joe's still at the Tamaqua, sleeping it off. Besides, you're doing everyone a favor. He'll be happy even to get the insurance money."

Liam hesitated, longing to connect to Billy, and reasoning that it would be ok. No one would know. Irish Joe would be happy with the insurance payment. He would do it. Without another word he slipped off the dock, reaching back for the jerry can and plastic wrapped matches taped to the side. The swim was short. He paused halfway across to look back at Billy on the dock, a gleeful grin of anticipation on his face, Super-8 camera at the ready.

At the barge, Liam mounted the dive platform on the stern and walked towards the bow, peering in the porthole of the wheelhouse as he walked by. He could see an empty cot, rumpled wool blankets spilling to the floor, empty bottles and cans overflowing. Dad was right. The guy was a degenerate, and the barge was an eyesore. He began to pour the gas from the can around the deck in a trail leading to the stern of the boat. When the can was empty, Liam looked across at Billy, who by now was holding the camera in his hand filming. *Filming*, Liam thought for an unsettling moment. *With me in the picture.* He hastily lit one of the nearby rags and tossing it on the trail of gas he had poured, dove off the stern, swimming underwater towards home.

Hours of playing tag in the water with his sisters had perfected his ability to swim underwater for considerable distances. When he resurfaced, more than halfway back, the neighbor Tommy McGuire was standing with Billy, watching as he filmed.

The bow of the barge was fully engulfed now, and McGuire was gesturing towards it, and Liam in the water. Liam pivoted towards the burning barge as if swimming that way. The alarm for the volunteer fire company was ringing loudly in the distance, and he could hear the far-off sirens of the FDNY approaching.

McGuire began to shout to him, apparently convinced that he was swimming across to rescue Irish Joe. "Fugeddabout it," he was yelling, waving his arms. "Da vollies are coming!" For a moment, Liam felt ok. Except for the file, he realized that he looked like the hero, swimming the canal to rescue the drunken Irish Joe. One more glance both ways as he was treading water changed his mind.

In one direction was his father, the instigator of this whole "adventure" grinning and filming as the barge burned. Billy had started filming as he poured gasoline on the decks, he realized, leaving evidence for all to see that Liam had committed an arson. In the other direction was Irish Joe, now sitting on a piling on the dock, head in his hands sobbing. *There was no insurance*, Liam realized, and he had just helped Billy burn down someone's home.

Liam swam back home, climbing the ladder to the dock, and storming angrily past Billy and into the house. The acrid smell of oil and burning rubber lingered in the air for hours, along with the more insidious odor of gasoline on Liam hands.

Some weeks later, on a field trip to the local anthropology museum, he spotted a wall full of African masks. The label described them as "West African, possibly Toma," a description that was at once enticingly exotic and meaningless. Each of them rested against a cloth backdrop in glass cases lining the dark Hall of Peoples, the solidity of their rough brown wood stark in the spot lighting of the case. Their elongated faces and vacant eyes were at once terrifying and familiar. Soon he was collecting replica masks, buying them from the museum shop, and later from exotic jewelry boutiques in Manhattan. The grotesque dark wood poses of the faces spoke to him in a way that nothing had since the blank spaces on the maps. He couldn't shake the image of the contorted faces, which eerily aligned in his mind with a picture of Billy on the dock, smiling as he watched the destruction that they caused together.

When it came time for college, Liam secured an appointment to Kingspoint, the Merchant Marine Academy. Though he hated the discipline, he stuck with it long enough to finish with a Mate's certificate. Shortly before his graduation, Liam returned home on leave. Billy was irritated that Liam was "parading around in his Good Humor outfit" (his academy dress-whites) and even more annoyed that Liam was unimpressed by the thirty-foot sailboat Billy had acquired. By now, Liam could legally pilot commercial vessels up to 100 tons. It wasn't this that made Liam wary of Billy's nautical aspirations, though. History or at least personal history, he believed, taught you all you needed to know. There was more than enough personal history for Liam to understand that Billy was incapable of operating a small boat with any discipline.

Billy's whims and obsessions would always make any boat he owned a floating navigational hazard, he thought. Still, when Billy proposed a trip to Bermuda on the boat as Liam's graduation present, Liam gave in. There was always hope, he believed. This time would be different.

By now, dear reader, you may be screaming inwardly. Or perhaps you are scratching your head at the on-going gullibility of the Quinns. The truth is more complicated without the benefit of emotional distance, and without the longing for trust that often comes from familial relationships. Liam deserves our empathy for his resilience, and for the spark of hope that remained at the bottom of the Quinn family Pandora's box of emotions.

The trip that followed ultimately became the stuff of family legend. It started with Billy picking a crew that included a co-worker with epilepsy who would forget to bring his medication, along with then 16-year-old Monica (who was small enough that Billy thought she might be useful if they needed someone to crawl into a tight space, and who would be suitably grateful to be included), as well as Liam and his current girlfriend, Lucinda.

Then here was Billy's questionable choice of coastal charts – automobile club road maps because they were cheaper and showed the coastal water. Finally, there was a storm, during which a sail jammed, inspiring Billy to send Monica, the smallest of the crew, aloft in a johnny chair to try and untangle the mess. Ultimately, they were adrift, with everyone stealing Monica's dry clothes and eyeing each other's food suspiciously. Billy blamed Liam, saying that he was a terrible leader, even though he wasn't the captain, retreating to his berth and remaining curled in a fetal position through the rest of the storm.

The Coast Guard cutter which eventually responded to their distress call promised to tow their boat to shore in exchange for a promise to never sail offshore again. "You're a menace," the captain said to Billy, shaking his head. Liam returned to the academy for graduation and soon afterwards signed a contract to sail as an able seaman on a merchant ship, vowing to put distance between himself and his father.

For the next fifteen years, Moira kept up a lively correspondence with him – mostly postcards of exotic places on his side, with only the words "love Liam" in the text box. She kept them all in a shoebox by her side of the bed, always wondering if the small bit of text was a command or a signature.

After the move to Flour Bluffs, Liam retired himself, and having met a woman in the Philippines, and reasoning that having his own family would insulate him in some way from the worst of Luna and Billy, he moved to Texas. Restless at home, and eager to earn enough to upgrade his yacht, he quickly began to run a boat chartering business, running tourists to Key West or Mexico. It wasn't long before Billy began nagging Liam to hire him on as a mate. Liam always resisted until the charter incident.

Liam had been hired on as a first mate to ferry a luxury yacht to Bermuda. Besides earning a hefty salary, he would be paid to fly home after, allowing him to vacation for free in Bermuda. Billy was relentless in nagging to be hired by Liam as well, and though Liam resisted, when the lone sailor quit at the last moment, Liam gave in. He would say later that it was the singular worst decision of his life.

Midway through their voyage out, the captain, a seasoned former lobster boat fisherwoman named Linda Laidlaw, told Liam that she intended to divert south to avoid the worst of an oncoming storm. Liam related the instructions to Billy when he came on watch to the helm late at night, only to begin an argument. "What the hell's the matter with you?" Billy shouted, "she doesn't know what she's doing! And what kind of a man are you, anyway, taking orders from a woman?" Liam may have been traditional (his wife was a Filipino woman, who deferred to his conservative views in everything) but he had learned the command structure at Kingspoint, and not following orders would lead to him not getting paid. Convinced that Billy was just objecting to be annoying, Liam ducked through the hatch to head to his cabin. Over his shoulder he said, "just follow the heading, I'm going to bed."

Several hours later, Liam was awakened by shouting. On deck Linda was yelling at Billy. From what Liam could hear they were headed straight into the storm. It was too late now to divert, and Linda was furious at the extra work and potential risk involved.

For the next twelve hours the three crew members worked furiously to head into the waves and keep from foundering. When they were finally through it all, both Linda and Billy took Liam aside. It was his fault for not being assertive enough (Linda) or for listening to his father above a lawful order from his captain (Linda). In either case, she intended to complain to the Coast Guard so Liam would take a hit on his mate's certificate. Countermanding a direct order was mutiny, technically at least. It was his fault for being so fascinated by a piece of ass that he couldn't listen to reason (Billy) or worse, why didn't they just throw her overboard and say she was lost in the storm (Billy)? The last was the worst.

Liam went to sea for the peace of the ocean and sky. The order and discipline of sailing gave him comfort. Billy's conniving and reckless behavior had put Liam in a position where he had to watch constantly to make sure that Billy didn't impulsively act and jeopardize Linda's life, not to mention Liam's career. The next few days were a non-stop marathon of watching Billy's every move, while sucking up to Linda to hope she would forget the incident.

When the boat finally docked in Bermuda. Liam grabbed his seabag and walked away from Billy, literally and metaphorically, vowing to keep to himself then on.

Several months later, Liam left with his wife on his yacht, determined to sail around the world.

It would be fair to say that before the event that Monica thought of as the "incident", her life revolved around the water. Since the age of five, she had been using a small skiff that Liam had set up for her to fish for crab in the bay nearby. Her independence had grown from Liam's confidence in what he taught her, Billy's indifference to all his children, especially Monica, and Moira's recognition of her intelligence and ability to plan.

Because of the separation in ages (Siobhan and Liam were seven and eight years older), Monica had become Moira's constant daytime companion, until she was ready for school. Moira took her everywhere she went, sometimes driving in her gold Ford Fairlane only just to get out, cherishing the time and letting Monica choose the route; "turn here, Mommy." It wasn't long before Moira could see that these were not idle meanderings; they were carefully choreographed journeys that Monica worked out in her mind before they even got in the car. Sometimes it was a trip to the drugstore on Flatbush for a chocolate egg cream and a Big Little book.

Monica read early and loved to sit with Moira as she read a library book or the newspaper. She always looked seriously absorbed in the adventures of Lassie, the Lone Ranger or a classic like *Journey to the Center of the Earth*. She had an ear for a story and a fine-tuned sense of what was logical for characters, even at a young age.

Though as for most children, Moira and Billy were the twin poles of Monica's emotional life, it seemed that from early on Billy had done his utmost to alienate himself from her, as if he were jealous of her bond with Moira, or even the attention she got from Liam and Siobhan as the youngest in the family. He was openly dismissive of her obvious intelligence, as well as openly hostile to almost any wish or ambition. Monica learned to read the lessons from these encounters with the intuitive grasp of an older child.

There was the time when he locked Monica in a darkened closet so he could watch a *Star Trek* episode with Liam. When Billy and Liam settled down to watch, ignoring Monica's screams and kicks at the door, Monica learned that family allegiances were flexible, and punishment could be swift and arbitrary. Later still, when Billy had spent hours watching Moira and Monica read together on a Saturday, an activity he found tedious, a furious argument erupted.

"Did you rinse down your boat?" Billy demanded. Monica immediately saw the question for what it was – a calculated attempt to short-circuit her time with Moira. He had never been interested in her boat maintenance before – leaving it totally to Liam.

"Later," Monica said, barely looking up. Billy was furious at the shifting alliances in his family, the sense that there was an inner circle that excluded him. He was also fuming at the idea that Monica wasn't his child, because by now he had begun to be certain of the gossip that he had himself created about Moira.

"Now!" Billy screamed, opening the deck door, and pointing, a vein bulging on his neck.

Monica rose and started out to the deck, irritated herself at Billy's impatience.

"You're not my father!" she said, under her breath. This was not truly what she thought. In fact, the opposite was probably true. She dreaded the idea that Billy was in fact her father, but with the keen intuition of a child, she knew this was a sore point.

Billy was beyond livid now. Looking around for a weapon, he spotted an oak paddle for the canoe leaning against the dock railing. Raising it swiftly, he swung it towards Monica's back, breaking it in two. Tossing the pieces to the ground, he walked towards her, leaving Monica lying face down on the dock wondering what had happened. "Just remember," he hissed in her ear, "just like

Joe Kennedy, I can put you away forever...on my say so, because I'm your father." This was a threat that he would repeat often over the years, playing on the Irish Catholic reverence for all things Kennedy, he used the story of Rosemary Kennedy who had been lobotomized and institutionalized by her own father, as evidence of his own power.

This story quickly became the stuff of yet another family legend: a chronicle of Monica's stoicism and Billy's blind, arbitrary and impulsive violence. In the compulsive re-telling and dismissal of this incident, Monica learned again that she was alone, and she saw that when the end finally came, it would be swift and total.

And then there was the final incident. It came right before The Move. Monica had been accepted to Cornell Engineering, a goal that might have seemed out of reach, but which Liam had encouraged. In the weeks leading up to the summer, the family had been preparing to move to Corpus Christi. Billy was in a low-level state of irritation at the inconvenience of it all when Monica stopped him. In one hand she held a printed form with the Cornell logo, in the other a pen. "Dad, can you fill this out?" she asked, thrusting both at him. Scanning the form, his face began to redden, "What's this," he snapped. "It's for financial aid...for college," Monica replied.

Everything about this exchange annoyed Billy, from the embossed Cornell logo on the heavy paper to the pleading look on Monica's face. She always made him look bad, like less than a father, he thought. One quick look at her face also told him what was next. She would gang up against him with Moira, Siobhan or Liam. They would dwell on Monica's accomplishment and offer reasonable-sounding compromises designed to make him look petty. Scanning quickly, he spotted a focus for his ire on the form. "This says 'yearly income'!" he said, jaw clenching. "That's private!"

Monica noticed that he was already slipping into full Brooklyn accent mode, a quirk that she had long thought was assumed when he wanted to emphasize his emotional distance from a situation. Here too it highlighted the distance between Monica's acceptance to the ivy-league and his own beginnings at an orphanage.

"It's financial aid, Dad," Monica tried to explain patiently, "they'll give money for tuition."

"I don't need no handouts!" he said, voice rising. Monica thought quickly, perplexed by his reaction. He was always first in line for a handout, she thought.

"It will make it a lot cheaper," she pleaded, "and everyone answers those questions, if they have parents." This last remark was the final straw for Billy. Crumpling the paper into a tight ball, he threw it on the floor and stormed away. Monica stood stricken. Moira bent down, picked it up and walked towards the kitchen. "Don't worry," she said, taking out her iron, "we'll fill it out together."

Later, Billy was bringing in the mail when he spotted an envelope addressed to Monica. Flipping it over, he saw a handwritten note on the flap, "MYOB Billy Quinn." We'll see about that, he thought, ripping open the envelope. He smiled wickedly when he saw what it contained: a steamy sex letter from a girl in Monica's class. Clutching the letter, Billy entered the kitchen.

Monica and Moira were seated close together at the Formica table. Moira had her reading glasses on and was reading the instructions on the financial aid form carefully. They looked up as he entered. Monica wondered briefly if he was coming to apologize. With a smirk he dropped the now open letter between them, on top of the Cornell financial aid application. The beginning of a particularly steamy passage jumped out at both. Moira looked stricken. Here was a thought that widened a gulf with Monica; wider than the distance to Texas, or the transformation that came with a pending Ivy league education. A world had opened that would exclude Moira irrevocably. Monica felt queasy. The girl who had written the letter had been pursuing Monica for weeks. Monica wasn't she had feelings for this girl and she was furious at the provocative note on the flap that had clearly been designed to anger Billy. More than that, she was humiliated that her feelings had been exposed before she had a chance to understand them for herself or talk to Moira about them.

Monica snatched the letter back, screaming, "you opened my mail…"

"It came to *my* house," Billy said.

Later, Monica could barely remember the turmoil that followed. She was ordered to leave the house immediately. They would be gone from Brooklyn soon anyway, but the pre-mature break was still hard. For several days she slept in a friend's car, before leaving early for Cornell and a summer internship. The family rumor mill took over immediately, morphing the story into a tale of open defiance, degeneracy, and intellectual snobbism.

Life at Cornell was challenging but Monica immersed herself in a daily grind of intense studying, classes and a part-time job in the cafeteria that provided a little extra cash and some meals. It was the opposite of all that the Quinns imagined, and it left Monica lonely and weary. The workload was intense, all-consuming. Worse, Monica felt all alone without the care packages other freshman were getting or the letters or phone calls. In a freshman English class other students openly laughed at her accent, effectively silencing her from then on. Still her hours in the library paid off with high grades. It wasn't long before the college recognized both Monica's promise and her financial need. They came through with a series of work-study lab jobs and grants that completely funded her education. Her classmates might have called her "that pencil-neck geek" behind her back, but it was said increasingly affectionately.

The years passed. Monica tried to re unite with her family once, for the baptism of Liam's first child back in Brooklyn but the cold reception from her siblings and parents convinced her it was better to stay away. The long silence between them was filled on the Quinn side with an escalation in the family legend about her. She celebrated her graduation alone and shortly afterwards, not ready to enter the job market, she accepted a funded offer to pursue a graduate degree at Cornell. It was here that Monica had her own stroke of bizarre good fortune.

Several weeks before, Monica had met a woman who caught her eye: D.A. Erhardt (named Dante Alighieri Erhardt, after the great Italian poet by her single German mother). Known to her friends as "Bella Notte", Italian for "goodnight", a commentary on her inability to to socialize past nine. Bella Notte was a psychology PhD student specializing in childhood trauma. she had grown up with her own legacy of trauma featuring a single artist mother, absent father, stints in foster care and finally a kind, though troubled stepfather. Psychology seemed like an easy, stable occupation but the truth was that she wasn't sure if she wanted to dwell on childhood, or the ugliness that the world could direct at children. Her secret passion was oil painting: landscape scenes of roiling seas, golden sunsets, and lonely vistas, all of them empty of people.

From the first Monica and Bella Notte recognized in each other a kinship born of empathy for each other's loneliness, and an appreciation for their mutual depth of independence. They moved quietly into a constant companionship and the shared vision of a life together.

The turning point came when Monica was working late at the lab on an experimental coating for the type of turbine blades that are common in jet engines. Monica was distracted as she combined chemicals under the fume hood, thinking about her upcoming dissertation defense and talking with Bella Notte on the phone. The experiment was not related to her research, it was just a test to help a friend. She paused as she arrived at a critical step, looking closely at the amounts of the chemicals she was about to add to the beaker. Was that a seven or a one? Shrugging inwardly, she decided that a seven was called for and began pouring. That's when it happened. Immediately, a cloud of bright green gas formed on the surface of the metal in the beaker. Monica slammed the hood closed, turned on the vent and watched in awe as the green cloud mushroomed to fill the hood. When she returned tentatively 30 minutes later, the beaker was gone, and a piece of shiny metal lay on the table inside the hood. Monica stared at the metal coating. After her defense, she would investigate it more systematically.

Once she had told Bella Notte that she couldn't just memorize chemical formulas – she needed to see them in her mind, rotating them in three dimensions. The coating that resulted from the "green cloud" was one such compound. When Monica had time to explore it, she found that it was a near perfect coating for jet engine turbine blades, increasing their efficiency by almost 30%. The patent that resulted allowed Bella Notte and Monica to move to New York city, marry (taking the last name Quinn) and within a few years to have two sons in rapid succession: Donell and Cody Quinn.

Together Monica and Bella Notte spent their son's early lives looking for ways to support or inspire them. Every conversation was a lively jaunt through politics, history, art and even spirituality. Their collective intellectual curiosity, confidence in their own ideas and love for each other was all that Monica's and Bella Notte's childhood had lacked.

Their stable relationship, their successful career lives (by now Bella Notte had given up on psychology and was painting full time) did little to mend fences with the Texas crowd. To be sure being gay had caused a rift in Monica's relationships with them, but her success and happiness made it worse. Though Monica was able to re-connect with Moira, and to even have her visit for important events in their children's lives, as the years went on Monica was increasingly a target of Billy's, and later Luna's wrath.

Donell would attend Harvard medical school, where he excelled at organic chemistry, as he would tell it, because his mothers had inspired him to memorize Pokemon evolutions. Anything else was easy, he would say. His abilities with chemistry in turn would lead him to pioneer a vaccine that would be pivotal in ending malaria in sub-Saharan African. Not long afterwards, Donell was appointed head of the World Health Organization. Worse, at least as far as Luna was concerned, he became a minor celebrity after a season long stint on *Dancing with the Stars,* where he became known as the "dancing doc."

His brother, Cody, would attend Yale law school, graduating at the top of his class. Though his passion was Russian history and economics, he became a top strategist for the Democratic National Committee and would himself be pivotal in the election of several important national politicians. Together Cody and Donell would joke that someday they would be President and Attorney General, just like the Kennedy brothers. Their biggest accomplishment to their parents was the their ability to embrace the world with trust, enthusiasm and delight.

The Quinn family north (as they liked to call themselves) may have been isolated from the Texas crowd but they were content with their lives and each other. Family legend continued to grow over the years, all of it calculated to suggest that they were aloof, uninterested in connecting, or ashamed of their connection with the southern Quinns.

It would be easy to assume that the distance between the older Quinn children and Billy arose because of the geographic distance. Corpus Christi was a long way from Brooklyn. Yet this was a fissure though that had been growing for years. Ultimately, it had nothing to do with physical distance. Omar Bradley's story, though it may seem out of order here, shows us why.

Omar Bradley, named in a spiteful mood of Billy's after the World War II general, was the youngest of the Quinn children. Though he hated the name, preferring to be called simply Brad, he had the same independence of spirit as the great man himself. Ironically, in many ways he was the earliest Cassandra among the children, having been forced to live in close quarters with Luna during their elementary and high school years. Early on he tried to tell Moira that Luna was not only different, but she was also determined to harm him and perhaps others. From a distance all the Others dismissed his alarm, reasoning that it was normal sibling rivalry, and that their parents would intervene. In the comfort of their individual silos, Siobhan, Liam, and Monica all assumed that any emotional distance they felt must have arisen from the physical distance, along with a natural tendency for independent adults to choose their own path. At the same time, they also tacitly assumed that the family gossip concocted by Billy they heard about each other was at least partially correct: Monica was a snob and a "man-hater", Liam was a non-conformist who was trying to flee responsibilities, Siobhan was too immersed in her own family, and eventually, Omar Bradley had disdain for them all.

Omar Bradley had tried to warn both his parents that Luna frequently stole money from them, lied and tortured family pets. After some of these incidents, Moira would confront Luna. Each time Luna's reaction was the same: a facial expression of studied innocence, often blinking back tears, along with an aggressive victim stance, fixating on details that were benign to derail the accusation, claiming it was all in the accuser's mind and finally, the master stroke, invoking family loyalty and cohesion. She was playing them all, he thought. Case in point, was the incident involving Luna's car.

Luna had a driver's license early: Texas allowed junior licenses at age 16. From the moment she was licensed, Luna began to nag incessantly that she "needed" a car: she would use it to drive them both to school, to run errands for her parents and to boost her extracurricular activities for her college application. Billy was reluctant until he was able to strike a deal with a neighbor who happened to be a car dealer. The brand new tiny red Ford Escort was waiting for Luna on her birthday, along with a list of printed rules in Moira's handwriting:

> "1) no driving after 9 pm. 2) no drag racing or mudding, 3) you have to take Omar Bradley to school and bring him home each night. If you break these rules we'll take the car away."

All of this so far might seem like a typical teenage negotiation, but what followed wasn't. Instead, it was a slippery slope of limit-pushing that devolved into a certainty on Luna's part that she was essentially in control, and on Omar Bradley's part that it might be time to get out.

One morning, the police showed up at the door. Luna had been out late the night before, past her curfew in her new compact car. Though she was also supposed to drive Omar Bradley back and forth to school, she often "forgot", stranding him somewhere. This morning the police were following up on a report from an incident that occurred the night before. A small car had been spotted on the side of the road near the shore. It was packed with teens who had been smoking pot and throwing beer cans out the windows and smashing mailboxes in a trail leading from a residential community to the parking spot. When the Sheriff's Deputy, Brian "Bubba" McGovern approached, they heard a young woman yell, "oh shit, it's the pigs..." before the car took off at high speed. To Deputy McGovern, teenagers drinking was one thing, but he had very definite ideas about how a young lady should behave and using language that would make his mama pale and hitting the gas was out of line. The rear license plate was also missing. He took off after the car.

Just ahead of him the car was weaving across lanes, traveling at over 70 mph, when it suddenly veered into a muddy track through the woods. He tried to follow but the narrowness of the gap between the trees compared to his patrol car and the high speed, made it very dangerous. He waited at the edge of the woods for the inevitable sound of a crash, but it never came. Deputy McGovern documented the incident, deciding to drive through neighboring housing developments in the morning to see if he could spot the car. It didn't take him long to find it, parked in the Quinn driveway, covered in mud.

The night before Luna had returned at close to 11 pm. Moira was waiting on the couch. Luna reeked of alcohol, was out of breath and began shrieking with sobs as Moira stuck out one hand for her to turn over the car keys.

"Why don't you ever listen to me first?" she shrieked. "This is all Omar Bradley's fault!" Moira had her arms crossed now, and one eyebrow raised, a sure sign of her fury.

"It was his friend, Richie," Luna whined, pointing in the direction of Omar Bradley's room, "who took my keys after Prayer Group and convinced me to sample the communion wine. He must have put something in my glass because next thing I knew I was in the car, he was driving through the woods..." here she choked back a sob, "and the cops were after us."

"You gave your keys to your mother," Billy said, "it will only be a week. We'll talk more in the morning."

"A week!" Luna screamed, gagging, and then vomiting on the floor near Moira's feet. By now Omar Bradley was awake and standing in his doorway, staring from one to the other, perplexed. The vomit on the floor reeked of vodka. Luna ran to her bedroom.

"Go to bed." Moira said to both.

Deputy McGovern was sure that he had found the car. At full daylight he had followed the track of the car through the woods, noting that it exited near Cabeza de Vaca Estates. It was also covered in mud, was missing the front plate and had a scrape mark on one side that matched a gouge in a tree along the route the car had taken. The elderly parents who answered the door were clearly confused though. Yes, it was their daughter's car, they said. Yes, the plate was missing because she lost it, but the mud on the car was because their son, Omar had stolen the car to go mudding.

"Where was your daughter last night at about 10:30?" He asked.

"She was home in bed." Billy answered, adding quickly, "after Prayer Group. Both are punished." Omar Bradley was listening in the living room. Fuming, he returned to his room.

"I have good reason to believe that you are either mistaken," Deputy McGovern said, "or lying to me. This is my patrol area and I fully intend to be on the lookout for this car. If I find out that it is involved in anything else, there will be serious consequences for your daughter." He walked away, shaking his head. Billy entered the house, took the car keys from where Moira had hidden them and handed them back to Luna.

Omar Bradley lay on his bed, looking at the ceiling. He understood that no matter what, his parents would defend Luna, even if it meant blaming another family member, including him. It was one thing for Moira and Billy to claim that Quinns had to stick together: but something else altogether if they were selecting who would survive. Worse, they seemed to have no critical ear for the lies they were being told. It seemed that as the lies became more transparent, his parents were also giving up the pretense that they were a family unit. The Luna team or no team, he thought. Rolling over, he went back to sleep.

Not long after came an incident that finalized his resolve. For years Omar Bradley had been complaining that Luna was hurting him, even when she was seated far from him at the dinner table. Naturally, when accused Luna would cry hysterically, dabbing at her wide eyes and saying that they were all cruel and that she was innocent. Both Moira and Billy were perplexed by these incidents, which suggested that Omar Bradley was not only vindicative against Luna, but he was also delusional. Afterall, how could Luna be pinching him from four feet away?

One night, at the table, Omar Bradley had been telling his parents about an accomplishment: he had placed first in a cross-country track meet at school. Luna was infuriated that they seemed impressed, not recognizing that Dance Line was much harder and way more prestigious. Kicking off her sandals, she stretched as far as she could and gave that nasty Omar Bradley a pinch in the balls. The only problem was that Luna's aim was off and 1) she had reached the fleshy part of Moira's upper thigh and 2) there was now no denying that she could pinch with her toes. The moment was not only painful, but a revelation to Moira. Now she wondered how many other times Luna had played the victim, and what else she had lied about. It was also the end of any peace between Billy and Moira. Billy firmly aligned himself with Luna in every family battle that followed, nagging and arguing until Moira gave up in disgust, retreating to the Manatee Club.

As for Bradley, he left home as soon as he could, joining the Air Force at the age of 16. After his enlistment was up, he applied to the University of Chicago, paying his own way with GI Benefits. His selection for Harvard Law School firmly planted him in the Others, especially when Luna announced at a family Thanksgiving that Bradley should call her Master, since she had recently earned her master's degree in Education (with a dissertation on using sock puppets to teach diversity). For once, Bradley didn't need to explain to anyone that his degree, a Juris Doctor, would win in any throw down because the Others jumped to his defense. Luna stormed from the house, snatching a cheese ball from Jimmy's hand as she went and pushing her twin sons Caster and Poleax towards the door. Billy raced after her, grumbling about sibling rivalry as he went.

When they had gone Moira and the Others continued as before, playing a lively game of Monopoly. They may not have been willing yet to accept the truth about Luna, but they were content to let the family drama play out elsewhere. Let Jimmy deal with it for now.

"No offense," Bella Notte said to Omar Bradley, during a break in the game, "but as a semi-outsider I don't understand why you all let Luna get away with some of this stuff?" Bella Notte and Omar Bradley had been close ever since he had spent time with the "northern Quinns" during Air Force furloughs. She respected his intelligence, energy and independence, and though politically they agreed on almost nothing, it was nothing a banana split, and a lively debate couldn't settle. She readied herself for a challenge.

"You're a psychologist," Omar Bradley replied, glancing towards the kitchen where Moira was loudly banging pots and pans, pretending not to listen "what would you do?"

"I don't know exactly, because she's not my sister, so that makes it different. I can tell you that she is openly manipulative and that won't end well for family cohesion, and especially for anyone who is left behind – like your parents…" she paused, glancing towards the kitchen as well. Billy had not yet returned from his trip to placate Luna, but Moira carried on indifferently cooking dinner.

"There was a nun that I met in grade school," she continued, "I was complaining about the daily grind of having to deal with some of the issues in my life as an excuse for stagnating. I'll never forget, she looked me in the eye and said, 'you can let people steal your past, but don't let them steal your future. You're the master of your own destiny.'" Bella Notte paused again, "You already did the first part: you got out and made your own life. Now all of you must let go emotionally. Find a way that you can dismiss her power over the family. She's really in a category by herself. Think of her as…Luna…" she paused, drawing out the name, searching for an answer.

"…Tic," Omar Bradley finished, with a jerking motion of the shoulders, a roll of the eyes in an exclamation that suggested that Luna was short for Luna-tic. They both laughed and it wasn't long before Liam, Siobhan, and Monica were all in on the joke, referring to Luna exclusively as "Tic." To be fair, Luna's middle name was not actually "Tic"— it was Lynn – and though this is ridiculous enough when you thought of "Luna Lynn Quinn," perhaps this might seem a kind of unfair bullying behavior often seen between siblings. You might now open a warm spot of empathy for all that Luna would endure. Yet if that is your inclination, you are as sorely mistaken as most of those who would ever meet Luna in her life.

Part Four – The Trouble with Conspiracies

"The trouble with conspiracies is that they rot internally."
Robert Heinlein

Billy was not an educated man. He did not have Moira's curiosity about the world, or any interest in events in history or culture. He was very interested in politics; not as an ideologue, but solely because of the whiff of power dynamics and the veiled threat of one group dominating another. When they moved to Texas, though, Billy had less opportunities for domestic power plays; partly because they had left the Others behind, but also because disturbingly, his relationship with Moira had changed. Rather than scratching his itch for domination within his own household, he began to delve into local politics. He tried various groups starting with the Klan, which he proclaimed to be "a NICE bunch of fellas," but which he ultimately rejected because they expected "$15 in dues!" Eventually, he settled on the local Republican club, delighting in the mean-spirited dirty tricks of local campaigns.

At home, Billy had time on his hands, but found that his grip on the family was slipping. It was now that he began to launch into agitated lectures, chiding Luna and Omar Bradley for their failings as children. To say that these lectures were unique was an understatement. Billy's tirades were a mix of literary allusions and historical facts. He had an almost encyclopedic memory for some obscure tidbits of history, most of which he got wrong. As the Others were in college, they often came across the original source for some of Billy's tidbits, only to realize that he had twisted them, or taken them out of context. When they would try to explain to him that he had gotten wrong, he would become furiously angry, asserting with arrogance that they didn't really understand anything. Later, the Others would speculate that this was one thing Billy shared with Jimmy: a lack of critical reasoning skills, and an arrogant conviction that they couldn't be wrong.

Most of these misunderstandings, and indeed, most of Billy's truly deviant behavior, revolved around a central theme: power. The gratitude parade that had to follow his unwanted gifts, usually acquired through theft: power. The ability to take them away: power. The interest in politics: power. All of these were essentially a power play within the family.

There were two bits of his schooling that had stuck with Billy, both from Shakespeare. The first was a pivotal scene in the beginning of *King Lear,* when the king decides to demand that his daughters express their love for him out loud before he divides up his legacy for them, pitting them against each other, and encouraging them to lie lavishly. This one he kept to himself, but he did claim that everyone competed. It was terrible "sibyl" rivalry.

The second was a clause in the Bard's last Will and Testament, when he left an "empty purse and his second-best bed" to his wife. Billy gloried in this idea, often claiming that they all should wait and see what HE DID when the time came. Monica patiently tried to explain the misunderstanding here. Modern scholars, she said, thought that the empty purse was an acknowledgement that no matter how much he had made, his wife was already an heiress. The second-best bed was probably an allusion to their honeymoon bed, and so was a loving acknowledgement of their sex life. "That's right," Billy replied, "it's an illusion. Shows what you know."

Everything also changed for Moira when they moved to Texas. The disability pension meant that she no longer had to work, and the change in location gave her lots of new ground to explore. New York was as familiar to her as a well broken in pair of sandals, but Corpus Christi was a shiny new pair of pumps. The two younger kids were in school and had begged not to ride the school bus until they had made friends, so the first task was to drop them off. But here was another change. In Brooklyn, she had made breakfast for everyone early, as Billy would leave often by 7 am. Once he was out of the house, she never knew what time he would be home, so dinner was a meal she had alone with the kids. Often, he would arrive long after his shift had ended, leaving Moira to take care of after school programs, homework, and meals by herself. She had learned not to ask where he went, as it always drew an angry retort. Without the discipline of work, though, Billy was often waiting at home. It was too much, and Moira found excuses to stay out all day.

Socializing had always been an important part of Moira's life, though before it had been a result of her various waitressing jobs or talking with other parents or neighbors in her kitchen. Now Moira joined the Manatee club, becoming active in the Women's Auxiliary, the Manatee Cows, and helping to organize fund raising drives for the Manatee Cove Elder Home. She also joined the local theater company, discovering a flair for the dramatic, and she signed up for classes at the community college; first in painting, later in finance and accounting. It was here she really began to shine.

On a Tuesday Wing Night, as she was tending bar, she got into conversation with a distinguished-looking man who was new to the neighborhood. Billy was home sulking, as he disliked bars, telling the kids self-righteously that he suspected that Moira was smoking up there at the Manatee. As Moira and the new guy, Chet (like Brinkley, he told her with a wink) bantered over the drinks she was serving, she discovered that he was a retired stockbroker. Over the weeks that followed, Chet came in often when Moira was at the bar, tipping her lavishing and giving her advice on stocks to invest in with the money. Eventually, Moira took the remaining contents of her secret jar and opened an account to trade. With her growing knowledge and confidence, the account grew exponentially.

Meanwhile something had changed for all of them. Billy felt the slip, blaming the Manatees and Moira's absence. He was angry at the change, but powerless to change anything. Over the next several years, Billy and Moira (and sometimes Moira alone) were constantly in motion; visiting the Others and grandchildren, traveling overseas with suitcases held together with duct tape to visit whichever of the extended family was abroad, or going on cruise vacations that they had gotten as a last-minute sale. Billy complained incessantly about Moira's other life, spinning tales born in resentment of her neglect of him (and them), her indulgence in a variety of vices. Mostly, they fell on deaf ears, but Luna saw an opportunity.

Omar Bradley understood early on that thinking about Luna's emotions made no sense. It was true that she could be cruel, but her cruelty didn't arise from anger; nor did her apparent delight indicate joy. Thinking about it later, he remembered two things.

The first was a family camping trip through Virginia. Family camping trips with the Quinns were brutal. Their tent was heavy canvas Army surplus with makeshift wooden poles and a distinctive and nauseating smell. Meals were white bread, peanut butter and fruit. Requests for any extras were met with "what are you, rich?" from Billy. Free time was filled with sights and activities that were defined by Billy's whims.

On one of the final days, they found themselves in a small town that boasted a tourist attraction with the irresistible name of the Caves of Mystery, as well as an irresistible family discount. Lining up at the entrance, the small group of tourists wound their way down a set of carved steps glistening with moisture, along an underground river in a flat-bottom boat until it culminated at the edge of the Bottomless Pit.

A plaque explained that the Pit was an abyss, an opening into the earth with no end. Tourists were invited to drop a rock into the hole, listening carefully for the sound of it hitting bottom. Omar Bradley shied away, appalled by the idea of an emptiness that vast, but Luna went right to the edge, dropping a stone and listening closely. She stood at the edge of the pit past her designated turn, her face frozen into an expression halfway between a grimace and a smile, eyes vacant. It was clear that she recognized something in this natural phenomenon – a kinship or affinity. Later, when Omar Bradley was taking a philosophy course in college, he came across a quote from Nietzsche that reminded him of this incident, "Battle not with monsters," he wrote, "lest ye become a monster, and if you gaze into the abyss, the abyss gazes also into you."

The second incident came much later, after her marriage. Omar Bradley happened to be at his parents' house when he overheard Luna on the phone, sobbing histrionically and speaking incoherently. Disturbed, he edged closer, ready to comfort her, but the call ended abruptly, and Luna turned to him and, with her face wiped clean of any trace of grief, asked him what was for lunch. The crocodile tears she had been shedding seemed to have evaporated, with no trace of her prior show of emotion left over.

As an adult, Luna's sphere of influence had broadened in several directions. First, there was her marriage to Jimmy. Luna and Jimmy were all in on the family thing, having five kids in rapid succession. The oldest were a set of twin boys, born barely 7 months after their first date, Caster and Poleax. Like Billy, Jimmy had a fixed and immutable set of ideas, many of them gleaned from his 8 years of Community College education. At the baptism, Monica had tried to stop Jimmy from giving the twins those ridiculous names, but Jimmy was insistent that she just didn't understand Greek mythology. With a sigh, he slowly and patiently explained that it was "an allusion to a story about the twin sons who are now the constellation Gemini. It's because they were born on May 15." "That's CastOR and POLLUX", she explained, stopping short as she saw Luna's face turning red and her eye starting to twitch. "Never mind," she said as she and Bella Notte drifted off to sit with Moira. "Wouldn't May 15th as a birthday make them Tauruses?" Bella Notte whispered, as her partner and mother-in-law elbowed her to be quiet.

Quickly bored with motherhood, Luna decided it was time to compete with Liam in the world traveling department. Nagging incessantly, she convinced Jimmy to accept a position in Russia delivering port-a-potties to the giant construction zone at Chernobyl. His latest company, the Royal Flush, was happy to send someone who could speak Russian to assist with their contract for the exclusion zone. It was only later that they understood that 1) Jimmy did not in fact speak Russian, though he had learned how to say "drive the porcelain bus" in a passable accent from a phrase book, and 2) that he had minimal ambition to provide any type of service and would spend every moment complaining about the lack of decent steaks in the country. It wasn't long before Luna was again pregnant, after a particularly intense round of vodka drinking, and they had to be what Jimmy described as "evaporated" because of the danger to the baby. Luna had the baby in Jimmy's native Greece, though he didn't have any relatives there, nor did he speak the language. When she chafed at the post-natal care, calling home to cry incessantly, Billy dipped into his savings to have them evaporated all the way to Texas by private jet. At this poing, Siobhan's big house in Connecticut next drew Luna's envy, and it wasn't long before she had convinced Billy to help them with the purchase of a double-wide trailer for their growing family.

Three children followed in quick succession: in tribute to Jimmy's mother "Lydia" and their Uncle Claiborne, their third child was given the name "Clamydia," which, according to Jimmy, was "a good Greek name." Fourth was "Zooy" (which Jimmy insisted was an alternate spelling of Zoe) and finally the baby, Oozy, whose name they insisted was either the correct spelling of Ozzie or short for an unpronounceable Greek name. All of them could have been poster children for family planning, according to Bella Notte, who Moira said had a "sharp tongue," since they were all born exactly nine months after an alcohol fueled event, like Taco Tuesdays (BOGO Margueritas at Paco's Downtown.)

For the first several years, Moira and Billy were heavily involved in the children's their care. Adding to the children's confusion, Caster and Poleax never recovered from the unsettling experience of being uprooted several times in their early years. When they returned to the US, they couldn't adapt to American schools, preferring to find their fun elsewhere. Moira and Billy were getting older and slowing down. It was challenging to have the constant care of five young children, and often easier to just turn on the TV, or give them money to play games at the arcade or eat at McDonalds. At times, days went by when their parents never saw them, as they were "focused on their careers." Billy and Moira never asked why they had to vacation alone or where they were in the evenings. The result was that all the children looked to Billy and Moira for important decisions, even slipping and calling them Mommy and Daddy on occasion. The children also quickly learned not to ask Luna and Jimmy for anything when they were more likely to get it from Billy and Moira. Meanwhile, Luna and Jimmy told their friends that this was the least their parents could do, because after all, they were retired.

Moira understood that the Spankendopoulos kids were different. They were much less independent than her own children had been, but they also had a keen eye for any opportunity to grab something for themselves. Though she was fiercely proud of her other grandchildren, the Spankendopoulos kids disappointed her since she felt almost as if she had failed as their second mother. The Others had all gone on to careers, interests, and successful lives. They turned their sights outward to the larger world, and their own families. Meanwhile Billy, and his favorite child Luna, focused on what they could get from within the Quinn family at large: petty power, the spiteful delight of pranking each other and always money. The Spankendopoulos kids feel easily into the pattern, having apparently inherited their mother's greed and their father's idleness.

During this time, Jimmy finally graduated with a degree in Solid Waste Management, which Billy secretly proclaimed to be "poop patrol" while proclaiming loudly to the Others that Jimmy's program was "very sciencey" and hard. The immediate result for Jimmy was a step up into a county job that included a real uniform, with his name stitched in red over the left shirt pocket, government benefits, and the potential for promotion with tests. (Admittedly, however, given his 8 years of experience with community college test-taking, perhaps this was not realistic.) As Jimmy saw it, the downside was that he didn't travel anymore, but the upside was the small janitor's closet he had fixed up as a man cave at the Plant, and the hours of overtime when he could nap in front of his small portable TV. Ultimately, this marriage should have been the achievement of Luna's life, her long awaited MRS degree. Even Luna recognized the gap between her expectations of marriage and the reality of Jimmy's actual achievements and personality. Jimmy's performance didn't disappoint Billy, though; he had learned to lower his expectations of his son-in-law. Jimmy, for his part, was delighted with Billy as the father he never had, reverting to a ridiculous adolescent over-sharing that included descriptive details of bowel movements that Billy would immediately share with anyone else who would listen. Still, Billy would make sure to introduce Jimmy as his "third son," to the annoyance of both Liam and Omar Bradley, because it was a status that was apparently so cheaply earned. Secretly, Billy even delighted in the knowledge that he was the locus of power in Luna's family: without his money, without his babysitting, and without his tolerance they would be nothing. He was also content if Jimmy kept Luna quiet.

Luna had used her bachelor's degree in education to get a teaching job in the local school system, beginning with a job as a first-grade teacher in North Bluffs, the district nearest to the more affluent Flour Bluffs. North Bluffs was nearest to the large military base and the children tended to be diverse, less affluent, and more vulnerable. Luna worked for the better part of a year, achieving mediocre ratings and no offer of a contract for the following year. For the next several years she moved from school to school, followed by rumors of "incidents" with children. Her fellow teachers and administrators could never really connect their feeling of unease around her to anything specific Luna did, but she just didn't seem to fit.

Then, in her fifth year of teaching, Luna began as a fourth-grade teacher at Davey Crockett Elementary. This time was different. For one thing, early on Luna invited the teaching staff to a Wing Night at the Manatee club. Once they saw the fun Luna with ten shots of tequila pumping through her veins, they winked at some of her odder behavior, the jokes that didn't quite fit and the stunning gaps in common knowledge, such as her confident assertion that there was a "South Virginia" or an "East Dakota." Then there was the support of Principal Wanamaker.

Principal Wanamaker had been the leader of Davey Crockett for almost thirty years. The local school board had left him in place largely because of his apparent dedication to the school and the children. Principal Wanamaker lived alone in a small house at the edge of town, spending every spare moment involved with school activities. There was no hint of a wife, or a significant other, but there were rumors of a secret life. Mrs. S had caught his eye to start with because of her flirty demeanor. She also seemed ready, willing, and able to do whatever it took to make him happy. He had his eye on her for Teacher of the Year.

Luna was naturally charismatic. Even the Others only gradually resisted the mosquito light glow of Luna's charisma, realizing that it was a mask for a yawning emptiness and a drive towards filling it with the pain of others. Luckily, as her family of origin faded into insignificance, teaching fourth grade gave Luna some things that she needed. For most teachers, tending to the often-demanding physical needs of young children is overwhelming. Balancing those needs with the needs of a family is even worse. Luna bellied up to the trough of students of Davey Crockett Elementary readily, overlooking the work of teaching for the delight of her power over a group of kids and their parents. Her classes quickly learned not to cross Mrs. S (she hated being called Mrs. Spankendopoulos) or risk her icy stare, or worse The Paddle.

It may be hard to believe that any state in the 21st century would condone corporal punishment, but Texas added a rider to a farm bill to do just that. Parents had to specifically "opt out" of letting their children be paddled by filling notarized forms in triplicate with the local board. The truth was that most of the parents didn't even know that the paddle existed, or that they had any options. Most students who were paddled were ashamed of the experience, and afraid to tell their parents. The small minority who told their parents, and whose parents complained, were handed the triplicate form, and sent on their way. At Davey Crockett Elementary the paddle hadn't been used much over the years; that is, until Luna came along.

Luna was delighted with the idea of a secret weapon to keep both parents and students in line. She also liked the idea that she was building a reputation as a disciplinarian who was feared by most of the students. Added to all this was the safety procedure requiring the teacher with the paddle to administer the punishment in the principal's office. This would ensure, it was reasoned, that punishment didn't get out of line for a teacher to enjoy too much. At Davey Crockett it was also an opportunity for Luna to interact regularly with Principal Wannamaker, showing off her best features.

The paddle itself was varnished wood with air holes strategically placed to improve its aerodynamics and to keep administrator's arms from getting tired. One side was inscribed with the legend, "Spare the Rod and Spoil the Child" in raised gothic script that would sometimes leave the imprint of an S on a child's legs. (Fourth grade legend claimed that it was Mrs. S' personal paddle, hence the monogram.) It hung on a hook in Mr. Wanamaker's office and because of the safety rule, could only be used in his presence. It was this that really brought Mrs. S to his attention.

Slowly at first, and then with increasing confidence, Mrs. S began to bring students for a paddling. Mr. Wanamaker always brought the student into his office along with Mrs. S, grimly handing her the paddle before taking a seat behind his large metal desk. The child would be forced to lean over a chair while Mrs. S administered 3-5 solid whacks on the back of their upper thighs. Mrs. S of course engaged in the correction with the vigor education deserved, bending forward so that her tight skirt stretched delightfully, revealing the lines of her thong and wiggling just so in the bargain. Mr. Wanamaker was glad for the new concern with educational discipline, and even more glad for the cover of his large metal desk. This was a new and unexpected delight that would stay with him long after Mrs. S had left his office.

Word spread among the students, and among the staff who took to calling Luna "Spanky" behind her back. Any jealousy they might have had was quickly squashed as Mr. Wanamaker began to rely on Luna for dozens of little annoying tasks, including spying on the other teachers. She was rewarded with a series of multi-year contracts, perks such as trips to the annual state education convention, and the best classrooms. It wasn't long before whispers started that Mr. Wanamaker planned to name Luna as the next Principal when he retired. But then the Batons came to town.

The Batons were a large, close military family with a long history in Louisiana. At their first PTA meeting, they were introduced as THE family that Baton Rouge had been named after. Luna disliked them immediately for their happiness, their closeness, and for the audacity they had for not caring more about their appearance. Each of the children, and even the parents, were large, or as Luna was fond of saying, "a heavy hitter." Luna ordinarily might have taken to tormenting their son Barry, a student in her class, by throwing out parts of his lunch when he was at recess or constantly changing his seat, but she was wary of the closeness of the family and reluctant to confront them directly. That is, until the day Barry returned early from recess and witnessed Luna rifling through his cubby. Looking up, they locked eyes, and she knew the only solution was to march him straight to the principal's office for a paddling.

True to form, the next day, the PA summoned Luna to Mr. Wanamaker's. Bettina Baton sat in the office, dabbing at her eyes with a handkerchief. Of course, Mr. Wanamaker stood up for Luna, arguing for the necessity of discipline, accusing Barry of stealing from other children, and generally dismissing everything Bettina said. As the meeting ended, he handed Bettina a triplicate form, advising her that it was always her prerogative as a parent to opt-out of the discipline program, though that was potentially to Barry's long-term disadvantage. All would have been well but for that fact that Luna was still flustered and stood to shake Bettina's hand, mistakenly saying in a sickly-sweet voice, "thank you for coming in, Mrs. Faton."

Afterwards, Mr. Wanamaker was caught in a pickle. Gone were his delightful paddling afternoons. He had to beg the board to keep Luna on, and promised to promote her to Assistant Principal, largely to keep her out of trouble. You might think that this unexpected gift of a promotion would please Luna, but it decidedly didn't. Her new job removed her from the classroom, lengthened her days, and forced her to interact with an unsatisfying group of adults: other administrators, teachers and parents, all of whom were largely unmoved by her charms and not in awe of her power. The job had become unsatisfying.

Even as a teenager, Luna blamed everyone else for her lack of perceived success. She couldn't really understand what she was supposed to feel, but she could see what she should act like. Early on, she set out to court her father, flattering, cajoling and begging in a never-ending cycle of need. For a while, Davey Crockett Elementary and Mr. Wanamaker had satisfied her needs. As things changed, Billy became her psychic ATM; punch a few buttons, and he would dispense whatever she needed most, be it cash, affection, or manipulation of her current victim. Luna's attentions made Billy feel complete in a way that no one else could. Her needs and victimhood started out small, but continuously escalated until one by one all of the Others, and Moira, stood firmly on the periphery of the family. As time went on, Luna found a series of witting and unwitting accomplices to her schemes of the moment, but it was now that she met her best accomplice.

Our Lady of Consolation church sat squarely in the center of North Bluffs on a block by itself. It was often called Our Lady of Convenience by locals who used their parish registration to get the trappings of Catholicism without any of the commitment – baptisms, weddings, or discount parochial school. The imposing Mission style church building had once served up four Masses on Sundays, along with CYO basketball in the church school gym and a food pantry once a month. Indeed, not long ago, it had been almost more community center then church to the largely immigrant population that surrounded it.

But while Billy had been raised in a Catholic orphanage, he didn't have much use for organized religion. He preferred, he would say privately, to worship the Sun god because, well, why not? Like many of his more outrageous positions, it was hard to tell if this reflected any genuine belief system, or if it was merely a contrary stance, the battle flag of a provocateur: designed to drop like a bomb for the maximum reaction. Billy needed things that made him look different. It was all about difference: the things that set the Quinns apart from everyone else, that made them a clan onto themselves. Freed from the need to conform, within a community of peers in a familiar neighborhood or at work, Billy was unleashed to the full bore of his eccentricity. These new opinions were cheap convictions, flexible for any situation. Billy might have yielded once to the idea of social convention and baptized all his kids, but when he retired to Texas he had completely given up on religion.

The rest of Billy's children found their way to their own compromises with religion, as well as other social conventions. Omar Bradley had re-found his faith while serving in the army and had even strengthened it by marrying an Eastern Orthodox wife. Siobhan remained Catholic, and religious; Liam became a Southern Baptist, and Monica and Bella Notte became Episcopalians.

Luna never saw any use in attending church until she learned that Mr. Wanamaker was a regular attendee. Eager to please him, and to present herself as the prototype of a good and holy woman, she began attending the regular early morning Mass on Sunday mornings, her family in tow. The "slam, bam, thank you Ma'am" service, as Jimmy called it, was mostly lightly attended, making it natural that she would get to know the clergy.

Father Theodore Krankenkopfer, "Father Ted" he would say with a smile, was new to Our Lady, having recently arrived from the Midwest. A mid-career clerical who had seen an opportunity for power in the church at a time when vocations were slim, Father Ted was polished at dealing with the public, even if his current posting would indicate his best years had passed him by.

The diocese was not happy to have him because of dogged rumors from his last five postings. In fact, when the diocesan Bishop received his paperwork, he wondered why there had been so many changes involving Father Ted over the years. Anxious to avoid problems, the Bishop sent him to the ecclesiastical backwater of Our Lady, hoping that he would stay out of trouble.

Luna legislated loudly to have her entire family accompany her on her new spiritual journey: an accessory necessary to the presenting the proper package, and a shield from any deeper questions. Billy and Moira resisted mostly, but the Spankendopolous wing knew better than to resist. An hour or so at Mass was better than the angry recriminations sure to follow if they demurred. Luna by now had been promoted, and was irritated that Mr. Wanamaker would probably retire soon, leaving her stranded in a dead-end Assistant Principalship. And then came the day of the annual church picnic.

Luna was late, having carefully prepared her outfit as something more provocative than usual: a pair of jeans shorts, and a linen shirt, knotted to show off her midriff. Father Ted, relatively new to the parish, was making the rounds, glad-handing parishioners. He was carrying an aluminum lawn chair that he would unfold by each long table, chatting and being "with the people, but not of them" as his last confessor had assured him was appropriate. Luna watched and waited, timing her arrival impeccably and abruptly unfolded herself in the Father Ted's lap.

Mr. Wanamaker, sitting across from the good Father, and Jimmy, also seated nearby were both startled. Looking them both in the eye, she threw her arms around Father Ted's neck, and wiggling her tantalizing lower portions back and forth cooed, "oooh, Father Ted, is that your wallet or are ya' just glad to see me?" Mr. Wanamaker flushed red, Father Ted stared stoically ahead, and Jimmy rose silently from the table to walk away. Mrs. Garcia, the head of the altar guild gaped at the glimpse of what Jimmy called Luna's "clovage" where a cartoonish 69 was tattooed on the upper part of her right breast, the result of another tequila night.

Surely, you might think, such provocative behavior in public is not possible. You would be wrong. Like Billy, Luna had long ago learned that crossing the line in a big way would make most people doubt themselves or even others before they would believe what some would call "their lyin' eyes."

Later Mrs. Garcia would shake her head, explaining what she had seen to her husband who assured her that she must be mistaken. Mr. Wanamaker would be sure that Luna was trying to send him a message: the afternoon paddlings had been orchestrated to hook him, luring him into something deeper. He would put in his retirement papers as soon as possible, leaving for Florida without saying goodbye. Fr. Ted, with his years of experience and education in female psychology, understood that Jimmy must be impotent, and Luna must be desperately repressed. In fact, everyone who heard about the time Luna gave the priest a lap dance had one of several reactions that the Others intuitively understood: 1) wasn't it terrible the ugly rumors that people spread about that lovely Luna? They don't know her like I do, or 2) you must have misunderstood what you saw. But Father Ted in true gospel style pondered these things in his heart and began looking at Luna with a new twinkle in his eye.

From then on Luna was inextricably involved in the church. She served on committees, organized events and insisted that Caster and Poleax serve as altar boys. Father Ted took a special liking to the twins, inviting them to the rectory for Saturday movie nights and driving them to soccer games when their team traveled. Luna was relieved to have someone take them away, liking the idea that Father Ted wanted to please her.

By now Mr. Wanamaker had left town, leaving Luna to adjust to the new principal, Señora Rojas. There was no longer the satisfaction of the game with the school children—the look of anticipation in their eyes when they saw her coming, the whiff of terror at the thought of the paddle, or the delight of condescending to parents who drove to meetings in brand new cars, instead of the used diesel Rabbit that Luna drove. She called them all by their first name, introducing herself as "Mrs. S" or "Vice Principal Spankendopoulos" and she made sure to mention her master's degree and her international travel. Her job was a daily round of reports for the SEN-YOUR-AH, as she liked to say in an exaggerated accent, and endless planning meetings. She was in a low-level state of anger all the time.

One Tuesday night, she was in the Manatee Club eating wings and sipping tequila when she saw the outside of Our Lady of Consolation in a local news story. Snatching the remote from behind the bar, she turned the volume up in time to hear, "…police are investigating the reports. The Arch Diocese declined to comment pending their own investigation." With a gasp, Luna rose from her stool and went straight back to her new double-wide trailer (a "gift" from Billy) to watch in private. Jimmy was already sitting in his favorite armchair, half-asleep with a beer in his hand. Luna snatched the remote from him and turned to the local news. The story was big news.

Father Theodore Krankenkopfer, the parish priest at Our Lady of Consolation, had been accused by an altar boy of a weird perversion. According to the young man, whose name had been withheld from the public because of his age, Father Ted had plied him with gifts and attention, gradually luring him into a relationship centered on administering enemas. Father Ted referred to this as "wash out", granting the boy special privileges and favors only if he participated. Eventually the boy had told his mother, who went to the police.

Luna's eyes rolled back in her head like a mako shark accelerating towards her prey. How dare that those little shits interfere with her plan? How dare that priest play games in her church? Jimmy's snorting laugh brought her back to reality.

"Well whadda you know?" Jimmy chuckles, "that priest hits from both sides of the plate – like he's amphibious or something!"

"You idiot," sneers Luna, "he could be doing your sons!"

"I never had no respect for no religion where the head guy makes no mistakes." Jimmy continues, "They say he's inflammable. But I bet that kid's parents sue for a pretty penny. Maybe we should call a lawyer." It was then that Luna caught a glimpse of her next move. Grabbing her keys, she headed to the door.

Father Ted had retreated to the rectory to think. Usually, he was a better judge of character, able to spin out his entertainment for a while longer. Somehow, he had miscalculated. The Archbishop had already been suspicious when he arrived, and was unlikely to fall for any spin. The options seemed limited, but then an angel arrived, disguised in the form of a very angry and disheveled Luna Spankendopoulos. Before she could raise her hand to pound loudly a second time, Father Ted threw open the door, causing her to fall headfirst into his arms.

Sputtering, she straightened up, looking him in the eye, immediately recognizing something.

They stood in silence for a moment, each of them bent on their own internal calculations. Luna saw it in all in a flash, a vision if you will. She could help him by lending her righteous, Catholic indignation for a smear on the One Church. He would be grateful and would help her with information. Father Ted had a vision too. A sexually repressed and bored woman, whose sons were already in his debt, he would dangle the force of his magnetism before her, leading her on to help him, and then when he had enough of the game, he would leave town. Each of them was confident in their ability to best the other, but the truth was they had each met their match.

When Luna returned home, Jimmy was perplexed. She had that glow about her that she only got when she knew she had already won.

"What happened?", he asked.

"Shut up, you idiot," she said as she drifted towards the wet bar to pour herself a large Margarita. "We're spending Thanksgiving with Father Ted."

His Eminence Cardinal Juma was cranky this morning, thought his secretary, Monsignor O'Doyle as he brought him his morning tea. The Cardinal sat with his back to the door, staring out the window overlooking the courtyard, his fingers tented across his ample belly. He didn't look up as O'Doyle set the tray on the sideboard quietly, awaiting further instructions.

Cardinal Juma was lost in thought, with many things to consider. Juma had served the diocese of Texas uneventfully for 20 years, relocating from Chicago on his elevation. As suited a "prince of the church", he lived in a hacienda style mansion complete with an Olympic size pool, hot tub and tennis court. Through the years, he had become accustomed to the luxuries that came with his job; not just the lavish house, but the chauffeur, the staff and the power. With the end of his career in sight, Juma had begun to wonder if it was possible that he might be elevated to the that last, greatest job.

The day of his ordination, at the age of 25, had been his mother's proudest day, but the days in between had passed in a blur from Monsignor to Bishop and then in a breathtaking flash to Cardinal. One of only approximately 200 Cardinals worldwide at the astoundingly young age of 55, he seemed certain to be on the fast track to some position of importance in the Holy See. But then… but then, he had stalled here, languishing in Diocese of Texas for all these years, staring down the barrel (a Texas expression if ever there was one) of mandatory retirement at 75. With that retirement, he would be relinquishing his right to vote in the next Conclave, which was sure to be soon. He was comfortable here to be sure. Not to mention that he had succeeded beyond his family's wildest expectations.

His father, Matthew Juma, had immigrated from Syria with his new wife in the 1920s, working originally with an uncle sharpening knives and selling chestnuts from a street cart in Brooklyn. The work was hard, and the winter was harsh. Worse, as Syrian Catholics, they had been in a religious minority, leaving for greater opportunities of freedom and in fear of the encroaching Turks. Most of the Syrian community in Brooklyn were Muslim, and though the Jumas traveled to Sunday Mass at Our Lady of Perpetual Help, they didn't really fit in with the Italians and Irish that made up the bulk of the parish. Matthew knew that the environment might not lead to much for him to leave his growing family. He also knew that the window for him to make a change was closing fast. So it was that within a few years of arriving in Brooklyn, Matthew Juma uprooted his family for a move across country to Dearborn, Michigan.

Brooklyn had been a shock on many levels to Matthew's wife, Fatima, and his family. The streets seemed perpetually grey and cold, and the neighbors unfriendly. Home in the tenement raising her young daughters, she longed for companionship, or at least relief from what seemed like perpetual cold. Dearborn did not improve the climate much for the family; if anything, it was colder and snowier than Brooklyn in the winter months. But the streets were wide, and their tiny house was filled with the light reflecting off the snow in the winter, and the green of trees and grass in the summer. Better still, the community church was filled with Syrian Catholics, and there was a place for two of her daughters, and soon the son who followed.

Thomas Matthew was, as it turned out, the only son. In keeping with traditional beliefs that a first-born son was destined to be a priest; Fatima spent much time tending to his faith. From the earliest age, Fatima read him bedtime stories from a leather multi-volume lives of the Saints that she had bought, and which assumed a pride of place in the only bookcase in their living room. He learned Latin early from an elderly nun at the parish school and served as an altar boy as soon as he could. His sisters (by now there were five Juma girls in all) might have been groomed for practical American positions as nurses and teachers, but Thomas was special. He was the one who would pave the way for the whole family in the church. Why else had the family even come to America to endure the cold, the unfamiliar customs, and the hours that Father had spent toiling in the local Ford plant? Thomas felt the weight of those expectations and believed fully in that future. It had been somewhat of a shock then when his father died unexpectedly when Thomas was only 16, and he found himself at Seminary early.

Thomas threw himself into all the Seminary had to offer, studying late into the night, praying, and ingratiating himself to a series of older priest mentors. Each of them in turn noted his dedication, his holiness, and his solid grounding in the faith. It didn't hurt that he was a member of an ethnic community, Syrian Catholics, who were an important minority in the church hierarchy. Here the machinations of church politics came into play. The Syrian Catholic community dated to the early years of the church. St. Paul had after all been blinded on the road to Damascus, but St. Peter himself was a Syrian had been their first Pope and the monasteries and religious orders were some of the oldest in the church. Surprisingly too, Syrian Catholics, while a minority, represented a solid 2% of the religious community in the country. For Thomas personally, the most important aspect of his Syrian identity was his "otherness" – his status as a fungible ally among the competing orders and nationalities in Mother Church. Every mentor along the way believed that by elevating Thomas, he was gaining a loyal friend who would owe him allegiance as he moved along the path to Vatican City.

It was no surprise then that he ascended the church hierarchy on the fast track: Monsignor by 30, Bishop by 40 and then Cardinal by 55. But here he stalled. As high as he had climbed in the American church, now he had achieved the status of what one of his brother bishops like to describe as a "horse in the hospital –you're not sure exactly how they got there," this bishop laughed about another prelate over cognac, "and you know that you must always keep an eye on them because you're never sure what they're doing."

The horse in question pondered this as he stared out the window this morning, along with the equally disturbing idea that perhaps his position was in jeopardy because of the twin inter-related pulls of early retirement and the budding sex abuse scandals in the church. Sex in the church was nothing new. As long ago as the Borgia Pope, there had been scandals of priests of all levels who had taken liberal views of their vow of celibacy. Over the years at every level, he had heard the whispers about other seminarians, monsignors, bishops and even cardinals who delighted perhaps too much in each other's company. A man of the world, Thomas had always understood this, viewing it as a natural consequence of a man's need for companionship. He didn't indulge himself, however, and turned a blind eye to the behavior among his brothers.

In the last few years, the whispers had changed to an understanding that his brothers were going outside, seeking companionship and solace among the people, even the children of the church. Worse, as Catholic family structure deteriorated and as parish revenues declined, family loyalty waivered. A mother with a concern about her children wouldn't tell the bishop; she went straight to the police, and sometimes even the media. Many of his brother bishops had been a victim of these lawsuits, costing their dioceses millions and damaging their Cardinal's Stewardship of his flock. Thomas knew that Rome had their eye on these cases, which Thomas had avoided until now.

This morning he was receiving a visit from Bishop Antonio Garcia, from the Corpus Christi area. Bishop Garcia was getting complaints about Fr. Robert Krankenkopfer, who it was now alleged had practiced some weird perversion with an 11-year-old in his local parish. The mother of this child had gone straight to the local Sheriff, a devout Baptist who was only too happy to

97

cast aspersions on Mother Church. Worse, the local newspaper was digging into Fr. Krankenkopfer's past, suggesting that his many lateral moves among parishes had a darker cause. All these years of an immaculate record, a clean slate so to speak, wiped out by an incompetent Bishop and a pedophile priest. There must be a way out, he thought.

His Eminence snapped out of his reverie as a buzzer rang, indicating the arrival of Bishop Garcia.

Moira had settled into her new life largely by avoiding her Flour Bluff family. She took classes at the Community College, visited Omar Bradley in Chicago, where he had settled after law school, Monica in New York, Siobhan in Connecticut, and Liam wherever he docked his boat. The years passed quickly. When she was in Texas, she worked a few shifts as a bartender at the Manatee Club, always saving some of her tip money for the day trading account to grow. And grow it did.

Her investment ideas were quirky, original, based on an odd combination of luck or timing and a powerfully intuitive grasp of group psychology. She sat one night listening to her friend and fellow Manatee Cow, Muriel, talk about her health-obsessed grandchildren, and the next day she bought lots of stock in Johnson and Johnson. She walked around a Walmart Super Center, spied a display of Monster energy drinks, and bought both stocks the next day. And everything she bought she hung onto, compounding her gains by many times.

As Luna courted Billy, hoping for more than her double-wide trailer, Moira mentally checked her gains, and dreamed of the day she would walk away to live comfortably and without drama with Monica or Omar Bradley. The doctor visit was routine, until it wasn't. Calling her the next day, the doctor explained that she had cancer. Her options were limited, he said. She should undergo radiation and chemo, starting immediately. Her husband and daughter, Looney (Moira didn't bother correcting him) would take care of her. Moira thanked him, walked out to the receptionist, and cancelled all her future appointments. She had things to do.

In the coming weeks, she planned it all out. First, she withdrew all her investments, putting them into a trust for the Others. She had spoken to a lawyer about a will, but he informed her that she couldn't disinherit her husband. Frustrated, she came up with a second plan.

Calling another lawyer, she devised a trust that would put Billy under the care of Monica as his guardian, and Omar Bradley in charge of administering the trust. Just to be sure, she would make Liam the back-up. None of them had love lost for Luna, who she suspected they called "Tic" behind her back.

Meanwhile, Luna had succeeded in rescuing Father Ted by launching a two-pronged attack. First, she used her position as head of the Daughters of Hera, the local Greek American club, to dig up dirt on his accuser. Years before, he had gone to Davey Crocket Elementary, and she had noticed then that the boy was a little *too* fond of art. As the investigation began, she called the hotline, and left a tip for the detectives that the young man was "light in the shoes," as she phrased it delicately, and suggested that he might be found cruising a particular beach nearby on Saturday night. When the police caught him in a round-up, she made sure that the item made the news. She also made sure to make an appointment with Bishop Garcia to deliver the news in person, in her role as a community educator and head of the parish Morality Council. In embarrassment, his parents dropped charges, leaving town. The next night, Luna showed up at the rectory again.

It was simple, she told Father Ted. She had gotten him off for now. Meanwhile though, she expected, well, information.

"Why would I do that?" he asked, "it seems like the young man has realized the depths of his sins, and repented."

"Has he?" Luna asked. "Well, it also seems like there may be other cases."

"Caster and Poleax told me everything," she continued, "and I have it all on tape. But don't worry, it will be our secret. As long as you give me information."

Speaking rapidly, she explained that she expected Father Ted to take careful notes at confessional, compiling lists of any information that he thought might help her in her new position as Vice Principal. Smiling, he agreed, recognizing that she thought she had outwitted him. It was a long game, he thought, remembering the bishop who long ago had taught him the nuances of chess and church politics; the first opening was assessing your opponent while they laid bare their strategy. Step two would involve planning your counter move, the final strike in the game. Checkmate.

Saturday afternoons and evenings were for confession, now called reconciliation by the Church, in a move to make the penitents feel motivated to bare their souls. Our Lady's congregation had been growing slowly over the years. Young families moving to the area sought a place to make connections, to find something traditional but new. Luna pushed Father Ted to promote the idea of some traditional practices, like confession, an eager shepherdess leading the flock into his corral. At first the confidences he shared were useless, annoying even, but then she had an idea. Now, when she met with Father Ted on weekends to collect the latest intelligence, she gave him a shopping list of individual confessions she needed. It wasn't long before she had her first golden nugget.

Señora Rojas usually didn't attend Our Lady, but she had traveled across town when her church was a priest short for reconciliation, and she was in a hurry for a quick forgiveness. Father Ted always arrived a tad late for these sessions, scanning the faces in the pews so he would be able to fulfill Luna's list. He didn't immediately recognize the older Latina sitting in the first row but was quickly able to glean from the details of her confession that she was a school principal, and that he had struck pay dirt when she mentioned Davey Crockett. Remembering seminary, he subtly guided the conversation into a more fruitful avenue. Señora Rojas, it seemed, was using money from the reading fund to buy buckets of Chardonnay for her book club; an activity that she justified as reading related.

On the next Monday Luna called Angela Crowley, a CPA, and the yuppie mother of a 5th grader who was dumb as a brick. Knowing that she was treading on fertile ground, she explained that she wanted to buy the latest trendy wholistic reading program for the school but confidentially was being thwarted by the principal. Luna carefully modulated her voice to suggest just the right amount of warmth and intimacy. "I wonder," she continued, "if you would be willing to spearhead a parent request for the program, using the money in the reading fund?" When Mrs. Crowley readily agreed (that Mrs. S really did have the best interests of the children at heart), Luna sat back with a smile to wait for the fallout.

Within days everyone noticed that Señora Rojas was not herself, snapping at the children, arriving late to school, and staying in her office all day long. It was then that Luna made her move, knocking on Señora Rojas' door, coffee in hand. Vulnerable and looking for an ally, Senora Rojas told Luna all. She had spent the $5,000 in the reading fund on wine. Now that evil Mrs. Crowley was suggesting that she should audit the discretionary funds at the school. Luna commiserated warmly. What if she could give Señora Rojas the $5k to replace the missing funds? They could buy the reading program, and then push Mrs. Crowley out of the PTA in disgrace? Señora Rojas felt the weight of the last few days slipping off her shoulders. Mrs. S reached into her purse and wrote out a check on the spot, drawing on her pension fund, she said. The truth was that Luna had already gotten the money from Father Ted, a small part of what he owed her. Senora Rojas was beyond grateful. "That Luna really *does* care about the administrators," she thought. "What can I ever do to thank you?" she asked. Smiling sweetly, Luna added that it would be a nice if she could park closer to the entrance. Perhaps they could trade spots?

Moira, meanwhile, had been somewhat astonished at how much her accounts had grown. Satisfied that the Others would deal with Billy and Luna, and allocate the funds among themselves, she tried to enjoy the months she had left, deliberately delaying any hospice care to give

Luna, Jimmy and Billy as little time as possible to change things before it was too late. One afternoon, as she was driving home from an errand, she happened to pass by Our Lady.

Though Luna was what Moira thought of as a "Cafeteria Catholic", consistently choosing to follow some rules, for example, but forgetting to mention her four abortions. Moira's faith ran deeper. The outside didn't really matter; it was inside that counted. Seeing the outside of the church reminded her of the comfort of Our Lady of Perpetual Help in Brooklyn – of the nuns with their beautiful singing voices, and especially of the nun who reassured her after her father's death by hit and run. She parked her car and went inside, heading for the confessional.

Because it was relatively early, there wasn't a line yet in the pews. Moira went right to the confessional booth and sat down. When Father Ted entered, he was annoyed that there was someone already in the booth, making it harder for him to guess who it was for Luna. No matter, whoever they were he would get them out quickly.

"Bless me Father for I have sinned. It has been 40 years since my last confession."

"What would you like to confess?"

"I am dying, Father. My husband is a petty thief and a bully. My youngest daughter is a drunk and she's married to a loser. The two of them have isolated me for too long from my older children. And now it's too late."

Father Ted stifled a yawn. He was in a hurry to get back to his bottle of cognac and his movies. Maybe he could move things along by cutting right to the penance.

"Five Hail M-" but Moira cut him off.

"I'm NOT finished. What I just told you is not a sin, it's a prelude." She paused."My husband is the most selfish person on the face of the earth. It's a fact. He's not overtly selfish – if you met him you'd think that he's a good man – he supported his family, didn't drink and, as he is fond of reminding us all, he didn't beat us. He's not overtly mean, but what's worse is that he does only what he wants, and makes it seem that YOU are petty to question anything. I've lived with it all over the years, bent over backwards to avoid arguments but..." she trailed off.

Despite himself, Father Ted was drawn in. He shifted in his seat, wondering who this was, remembering that once, long ago, connecting with parishioners had meant something to him.

"Go on," he prompted quietly.

"My own father was a Lutheran, and he carried in his wallet a clipping from a paper, an editorial written in German by a Pastor named Neimoller. The editorial was about how this Pastor stood by while the Nazis rounded up communists, criminals, socialists, Jewish people, and so on. Each time, he didn't speak up, because he didn't belong to those groups, and by the time they came for him, it was too late. There was no one left to speak for him." Moira was silent for a moment, gathering the rest of her thoughts.

"We've had it pretty good, and I don't think anyone is coming for us. That's not what I mean, but it's too late for me. I allowed Billy to do what he wanted, even when I thought it was wrong, because it was easier, and I thought I would have time later to make it right. Or, transparently, that he would die first, and then *I* could make it right. Now I'm out of time, and worse, I can see that he is going to let my daughter take over. I spent some time in the last few years taking college courses, and it's been wonderful – I've learned so much. The finance courses I took allowed me to understand investments, and my bank accounts have really grown, but the psychology courses I took were scary. They made me understand that Billy and Luna are sociopaths..." here she stopped because of the gasp from the Father. She wasn't sure, but she believed that a priest was not allowed to comment on particular people by name.

Father Ted, meanwhile, had been listening closely, perhaps for the first time in years. The woman's story was poignant, but two things had pulled him up short – first the mention of investments, and large sums of money, and then the mention of Luna's name. This was the prize he had been looking for, the golden nugget that finally would free him from her grasp and get him out of the country for good. The gasp was involuntary.

"Forgive, my child." He said. "Please continue, it must be awful for you…"

Father Ted hoped to get as many details as he could about the accounts before he could form a plan. He could sense, though, that she was second guessing her time here, and that it might be too late. He also sensed that this might be his only chance to get the information he needed. Moira had indeed begun to regret her decision to come here, and she was certainly not going to say anymore. In the few seconds of silence, she thought through her options, and decided to leave. Opening the door, she walked down the aisle and out of the church. She hadn't stayed long enough for penance or absolution, but that was fine. Not because she didn't believe, but because she didn't want to be talked out of what she was about to do.

Getting back in her car, she traveled straight to the office of Fidelity, changing her account to payable on death to Monica. She knew that Monica would divide the money fairly between the Others, and she would try to tell her about the account before it was too late. Changing her Will would be impossible without letting Billy and Luna know, and besides, there was more than enough money in the investment account to leave a generous settlement to all the Others. Somehow with the decision made, the pain in her leg was worse. She would go home and tell Billy about the cancer, then she would call the doctor for herself. Maybe it was finally time for hospice.

Father Ted listened to the sound of the door closing and the footsteps retreating out of the church. Perhaps it would have been best spiritually to go after the woman, bring her back to the confessional or the Rectory for a chat. She would repent, accept a penance and absolution, saving her soul and easing her last days. But this, this was a sign from God. Instead, she had willingly left, forgoing repentance, and opening the door for Father Ted to do what he saw fit. Into the bargain, she had walked past waiting parishioners. Most of them wouldn't know her and that could work to his advantage later. For now, he had to decide how to deal with the information he had as it related to Luna.

Once Moira had decided, things moved quickly. Surprisingly, Billy was distraught and angry when she told him. Not surprisingly, his dismay was all about him. What would he do now? Who would take care of him? How selfish could she be? Moira was tired of dealing with a lifetime of Billy's nonsense. Wearily, she picked up the phone, and began arranging for hospice services. Telling the Others was harder. They were all concerned about her, and shocked that the mother who was always so strong was counting down the days. All of them planned to visit her, to Billy and Luna's annoyance. A steady stream of adult children and grandchildren arrived, wanting to sit with Moira and chat or read her a mystery novel. Billy resented the upheaval, and quickly asked Luna to take charge. Luna was more fun, Billy explained to Moira.

Meanwhile, Fr. Ted had thought through the implications of what would happen next. This was special information, he was sure, and information that would lead to his own exit strategy before the hounds found him. The next day, before Moira had even told Billy, Fr. Ted had told a version of the story to Luna, warning her that they had to proceed carefully to ensure that no one else knew what they were doing. "Remember," he said, "it's important not to get anyone riled up. If they're angry at you and they see a hole in the strategy, especially before Moira dies, we're screwed. This is the long game. It starts with transferring all the money to her loving husband. Then you must spend the next few years caring for him, and slowly, slowly draining the accounts to hide the money. It won't work, though if they're at odds with you, or if they believe that you could screw them. The best disguise is always a camouflage. Blend into the family because nobody remembers a mirror."

At first, Luna tried to play the dutiful daughter to Moira. She brought her plates of food and sat at her side. Everyone, especially Moira, found this annoying. It was too drastic a change from the fiercely independent mother who took care of everyone else. Worse, it was out of character for Luna's relationship with Moira. Through the years, neither had cultivated a nurturing relationship. Luna knew she needed to take charge and keep an eye on everyone that visited Moira but she could barely contain her resentment at her new role, allowing it to seep into her tone of voice and the infantilizing way she approached every decision. Moira quickly told Luna that she needed to find a new hobby, and the hospice nurse that she needed an extra dose of morphine.

Soon she was in a delightful haze, watching events around her with detachment, wondering vaguely why that annoying nurse with the fake southern drawl, the ridiculous name (who names a child Moonbeam?) and the dumbass husband kept bothering her. TV became too much to follow. She entertained herself by throwing handfuls of bills and small change on the floor to watch Moonbeam's children dive for them and fight each other. Her father, killed long ago by a drunk driver, tossed his hat in through the door, just as he had once with her mother. She knew better than to throw it back out, leaving it to lie at the foot of her recliner where no one seemed to notice it. He smiled that glittering Irish smile at her, winked, and went to stand in the corner. *Don't worry*, he whispered, *I'll be waiting for ya right here when you're ready.* Who are these people, she asked when Moonbeam had just tried to force feed her apple sauce. *Never you mind*, he said, *just think about Monica, Siobhan, Omar Bradley and Liam. They're the ones of your heart.*

After a few weeks, Luna and Billy had enough. They needed to get on with their lives; to make the others go away once and for all. Luna began upping the morphine and Billy told the Others it was time for them all to go. She doesn't want you here, he said. She wants you home with your families. And one by one, they hugged Moira and left.

Sometime before, Luna's oldest sons, Caster and Poleax, had followed in her footsteps by enrolling in Ole Miss. Everyone suspected that the twins were not really college material, especially considering their DNA, and that they would follow their father into the so-called "poop patrol." The truth was, though, they had their father's work ethic, and so they readily embraced the idea of going far away from home to revel in beer pong parties and cold pizza breakfasts as long as it might last.

Within a few weeks, they plunged headlong into the college fraternity scene by joining Sigma Delta Mu. SDM was known to local wags as the "human sacrifice" frat after a brother, high on bath-salts, accidentally killed a pledge during a hazing ritual by setting up a huge cauldron and cooking him alive. The event, billed as "a Trip to Cannibal Islands hosted by Jeffrey Dahmer" had included copious amounts of alcohol for pledges, some of whom had to sit in the "cooking pot." The pledge in question, wrists bound together, passed out after consuming almost a whole handle of vodka through a funnel. Later attorneys for SDM pointed out that the young man would have probably died anyway from alcohol poisoning, even if the brothers hadn't forgotten that they had something "on the stove." The callousness of this remark went a long way towards tipping the jury towards convicting the senior brothers. They were expelled from Ole Miss and ultimately served jail time but SDM emerged largely unscathed. The investigation and university suspension that followed had only resulted in a brief pause in recruitment, though it had considerably enhanced the frat's reputation among the "knuckle-head crowd," as one Dean was fond of pointing out.

During the next rush week the expectations for entertainment at Sigma were unusually high, causing Caster and Poleax to call home to Jimmy for advice. He was, they both knew, an expert at entertainment.

"Why not do a menstrual show?" Jimmy proposed. When their silence affirmed that they didn't have his enormous vocabulary, he explained.

"You know," he said impatiently, "when you paint your face black and sing and dance like an idjit?"

Caster and Poleax were immediately all in. Unfortunately for their college careers, 1) a frat brother posted the hilarious pictures on Instagram, 2) the Dean of Diversity, a stern Jamaican woman with no regard for what the twins insisted was merely "Southern tradition," was not amused. Worst of all, they had the bright idea of invoking their Uncle Omar Bradley, the Harvard lawyer, who was also not amused and was quick to tell said Dean that the twins were "dead to me." Of course, this last piece was all that would remain of the story in family legend, as Luna was quick to tell all who would listen that Omar Bradley had conspired to ruin her son's college careers. For now, though, Luna had them home again and would keep them busy babysitting their grandmother and keeping the Others away.

Luna was finally in charge. During the day, she sat at Moira's side, pinching her occasionally just to remind her who was boss. As an extra little piece of fun, she went to Target to buy as many old Shirley Temple movies as she could find on DVD. Moira had a horror of the cutesy poverty and gleeful resilience of Shirley Temple. Luna made sure that they were constantly playing on the TV. But Moira seemed far away now, and Luna was disappointed that she didn't see much of a reaction. It would show that nasty Monica, and Omar Bradley too. Both had yelled at Luna for choosing the Shirley Temple movies. What did they know, anyway?

On the fourth day, Fr. Ted came to administer last rites, and was shocked to see how far away she had slipped. Taking Luna aside, he asked if she had the account number for the stock account and had gotten Moira to sign it over to Billy. Luna tried to play it cool, but the truth was she had forgotten that step in her annoyance at the Others. Squinting one eye, a habit she when she was thinking hard that reminded everyone of Popeye, she lit into Fr. Ted.

"How am I supposed to remember everything?" Luna screamed. "The woman is so zonked out now, we'll just have to wait."

"You don't understand," said Fr. Ted. "If she made that account payable on death, we're in trouble. It could be payable to anyone, even Monica or Omar Bradley. Tell her what she wants to hear. Then take her to the investment firm and have her sign the money over to Billy. We'll get it down the road."

That very evening, Luna let the dose wear down a bit, then stood just behind Moira's left ear.

"The papers," she whispered, "Monica needs the papers. Where are they?"

Moira looked up. Her father was standing in his usual place, a concerned look on his face. He must be worried, she thought, about the papers. "Over there," she said to him, pointing at a plastic bin full of her favorite Irish sweaters. "That's where they are."

Luna made sure that the overnight nurse knew that the dose was not strong enough. Then later, when Moira was asleep, she came back in. "Good," she said to the nurse in apparent relief, "she's asleep. I wanted to have these sweaters cleaned, so that she can give them away," taking the bin into the living room. When she found the account information tucked into the pocket of a cardigan in the middle, she almost screamed in delight. There was far more money here than she thought, several million dollars more, in fact. How dare Moira keep this from them? She needed to talk to Fr. Ted right away.

Luna's meeting with Father Ted, or simply Ted as she was calling him now, had the uncomfortable feel of a dance between two partners who are constantly sizing each other up. Ted knew too that he might have missed an opportunity by not chasing Moira. Perhaps if he had, he might have been able to garner the entire account as a donation to the church. But then a donation of that size would surely have drawn the wrong kind of attention. Better to work with Luna, let her think that he was working with her, leaving her with a target on her back. One thing was certain: with the slight gleam of sweat on her forehead and the glimpse of her tattoo, Ted felt a stirring that was familiar. Perhaps she would be useful for even more than simply money. Or perhaps, he thought with condescension, he could manipulate her need for him as well.

Luna also had doubts. What use was Ted now, anyway? Perhaps it was time to distance herself. She had gotten all the intel from him she could, along with the changes she needed at school. Ultimately, it was annoying to have so many stupid, needy men thinking they were calling the shots: Billy, Jimmy, and now Ted. He had been useful, but perhaps it was time to move on. Or maybe she could use him – get his help to grab all the money, then leave him with a target on his back.

Ultimately, the plan was simple. Work with the drugs to get Moira to transfer the account to Billy. Luna and Ted knew that he was not as smart as he thought he was, and both were confident that they could manipulate him. When Moira was gone, they would use the last few years of Billy's life to drain the accounts and transfer money until it was all theirs.

That afternoon, Luna was alone with Moira. She had just fed her lunch, keeping up a steady stream of baby talk as she worked, knowing that it would have been profoundly irritating to Moira, if she wasn't helpless to stop it. "Does the Princess want another scoop of ice cream? Open your mouthy, wouthy, baby girl. It's an airplane coming…" Luna paused, the baby talk beginning to irritate even her. How could Moira be so selfish to put her through all this? Screwing up her face in a pout, Luna pinched Moira as hard as she could. "Wakey, wakey. It's time for a talky walky."

Moira heard a voice from far off. Drifting in a haze, she wondered idly who it could be. She hated the state she was in now, lingering here between worlds. She had wanted to leave when Monica and the Others had gone home to their families. For a second time, she felt betrayed by her body: stuck with Luna and Billy and the grubby grandchildren with absurd names, unable to move into the light that beckoned. The last few years had been occupied with travels up North to visit the other grandchildren. None of them seemed to want anything from her beyond her company. A return home always meant disappearing down a slide into the yawning maw of Spankendopoulos needs, which had now reached a fever pitch. If she kept her eyes closed, maybe Luna would lose interest as she usually did, moving away to convince everyone how hard this was on her. It was then the whispers started. A voice was telling her that the plan was all wrong. "Listen," the voice said in a rasp, "you made a mistake. Leaving it all to the Others means that The Government will step in and give it to Billy anyway. He's the spouse. The only solution is to leave it to him and sign a new will. He will make sure later that everyone gets their fair share."

Moira peeked through half-open eyes. Luna was nowhere to be seen. Moira's father sat comfortably in the corner, staring at a spot just over her left shoulder. Yes, she would do what he was telling her. Later, when the haze had lifted somewhat, Luna came in with Billy who lifted her up and carried her to the car, propping her up in the backseat. The outside world passed in a blur before Billy lifted her again, putting her in a wheelchair and pushing her into an office.

The man behind the desk, dark hair slicked back, muscles bulking against his tight suit, seemed vaguely familiar. He was talking to Billy and Luna as if she wasn't there, arguing in whispers about her "capacity." Luna's voice was rising, telling the man that her parents were

113

elderly and "in love" – they were devastated at their impending separation, and it was all falling on her to keep the family together and to care for them. She started to dab at the corner of her eyes theatrically with a Kleenex she had grabbed from the man's desk. Moira's eyes began to close, and she felt herself slumping towards the wood of the man's desk.

Luna threw an arm around Moira's shoulders, grabbing the back of her blouse to keep her steady and said loudly, "don't worry, Mommy…Mr. O'Malley is taking care of us. HE HAS SOME PAPERS FOR YOU TO SIGN."

Doubtfully, Mr. O'Malley put some papers in front of Moira, pointing to a signature line as Luna placed a pen in her hand. Moira smiled knowingly and bent to her task, her father whispering in her ear, "it's the pigs at the trough, me girl." Looking over at Luna, Moira carefully inscribed an oval with a snout and a curly tail, pleased with her spontaneous artistry.

Reddening when she saw what she had done, Luna snatched the paper from Moira's hand and tore it in pieces. Demanding another, she held Moira's hand as she scribbled M. Quinn. Mr. O'Malley looked anxiously at Luna.

"I didn't fill it in yet," he started to complain as Luna leaned forward menacingly.

"It will do" she said, in her best Vice Principal voice, "or do you intent to keep my ELDERLY parents waiting here even longer?" Turning to wheel Moira to the door she continued, "bring a copy out to the car, please."

Moira wasn't sure what had just happened and was starting to make small squeaking noises. Her father was shaking his head and making menacing gestures at Luna. Billy was staring into space as he followed them both.

Back home, the afternoon light flickered off the water of the canal, playing along the ceiling over Moira's head. One eye was stuck open as the hospice nurse shook her head at Luna dragging her outside.

"Don't you judge me! The trip was necessary," Luna said to the annoyed nurse, "she wanted to see the water for the last time."

The haze grew deeper as the nurse upped the morphine dose and settled Moira back in bed. Ahead of her, Moira could see a deep blue sea and her father standing on the deck of a beautiful yacht, waiting to leave the shore. She stood up, surprising herself by stepped nimbly onto the deck, all pain gone now. Her father turned to her smiling from his position at the captain's wheel.

"Blue waters," he said with a wink.

This should have been Luna's moment; her chance to soak up the well-earned gratitude of all the Others, and of Billy and Jimmy for all she had done to arrange things. After all, for the past few months, she had to make the nurse/attendant schedule, take charge of the funeral arrangements, the lawyer stuff, manage the Others, and Billy. Omar Bradley had repeatedly tried to interfere, insisting on sitting with Moira, and taking turns with Monica to make sure that Moira was comfortable. Eventually, Luna had told Moira they were both about to lose their jobs, forcing Moira to urge them to return home. For the next few weeks, Luna had Caster and Poleax start moving furniture and valuables out of Moira's house to her double-wide trailer whenever Moira was sleeping. And now that the funeral was finally here, all the Others were complaining again.

Moira hadn't "wanted" a funeral, according to them. She had insisted on being cremated, her ashes to be kept in an urn. She had even picked out the urn, an inlaid cedar box with a sailboat inscribed on the front. Now that the Princess was gone, Luna had to endure weeks of arguing with Billy to get him to agree to a few simple things: a Greek funeral with the local Patriarch presiding, and an enormous blue and white ceramic urn with an Orthodox cross painted on the front.

At first, Billy had protested that Moira was *Irish*, and that a Greek funeral didn't make sense. Scrambling, Luna explained that Jimmy was distraught – he had thought of Moira as if she was his mother. Really, Luna had two motivations. A Greek funeral would be useful in cementing a connection with the new Principal, a formidable woman named Dimitra Spetseri, who had a flair for the dramatic and who had taken Luna under her wing.

Principal Spetseri was determined to help Luna mourn her beloved mother without those "nasty relatives" who were taking advantage of the poor girl. The funeral would be the traditional "100 Days" service and wouldn't include any of the Others, which was a secondary motivation for Luna. She would be the center of the Show, a public display of her status as dutiful daughter and of the family's gratitude for all she had done. The interment would have to wait until Billy died, when Luna had already decided that the urn would be placed between Billy's legs, where Moira belonged, and buried with him in the veteran's cemetery up north, near the Others.

For now, she would take over with Billy, installing Caster and Poleax in his house to keep an eye on him, and transferring the checking accounts to her name. It was then that she would really start rewarding herself, buying a few things to compensate for all she had done. Billy wouldn't notice or care, if she fed his childish desire to have fun.

There was one scary moment when Omar Bradley called, lawyer that he was, to ask about the will.

"She left it all to DaDa, you selfish prick", Luna shrieked, beginning to sob, as Billy rushed into the room the room to comfort her. Snatching the phone from Omar Bradley, Billy intoned calmly, "Anyone who is against Luna is against me," before hanging up abruptly. As quickly as she had begun to wail, Luna pivoted to a whole new emotional stance – the aggrieved and misunderstood dutiful daughter.

For the first few months of his widowhood, Luna kept Billy busy with a whirlwind of doctor's appointments, gym classes for seniors and family events. The work of the arrangements was hard, but the actual management of Billy was left to a rotating staff of her children, and Jimmy, all of whom knew better than to cross her. Partially, this set the tone. Luna was the center of fun; the one that Billy could depend on. It was also set at a frenetic pace designed to make Billy ask Luna to slow down, setting the stage for leaving him alone *because that's what he wanted.*

In the months that followed, Luna went shopping. She was clever enough to understand that it had to be a gradual process. The Others were attentive to her treatment of Billy, but especially of the way he favored her. She knew they were jealous of her success, so bit by bit she would drain the accounts by buying herself and the family lavish gifts. If Billy lived longer than she expected, eventually there would be nothing left, and she would call the Others crying that Dada is too much and needs dedicated nursing care. When they agreed that she needed a break, she would transfer Billy to the nursing home on Route 19. It would mean giving up his pension, which she collected every month, but by then all the real assets would be gone, if she could come up with a plan. The first step was the house. How selfish it was of Billy and Moira to force her and Jimmy to live in a double-wide when they had a big waterfront house to themselves. She would have to fix that.

Jimmy might be impatient, but she knew better. There was a scary moment when she realized that the nasty Monica was still calling Billy, and even leaving messages on his answering machine. Monica had urged Billy to "spend it all on himself" and "get a girlfriend." Luna fixed that quickly enough. She turned the ringer on the phone way down, forcing them all to leave messages for Billy, and then having Jimmy go by once a week to erase them all.

Later still she gave Billy a tablet with a recording device installed, for any interactions she might miss. It lay in the living room gathering dust since Billy didn't really understand what it was, but always fully charged and recording every phone call and conversation. The click tracker on Billy's computer turned up little beyond Castor and Poleax's fondness for the "Spank and Drain" porno site. Luna was furious that those two idiots installed the tracker to start with, and then forgot it was there. In a rage, she punched them both in the back of the head. "Didn't you two have enough with Father's fun and games?" she asked.

Thinking of Father Ted made Luna pause. It had been several months since they had been to Mass, and even more since she had contacted him. Ted was certainly falling behind on his obligations to her. There hadn't been new information from him. Maybe it was time to find a new way to deal with Principal Spetseri, or even Jimmy. Tonight was Taco Tuesday at the Manatee. Even though Moira was long gone, she would stop by, pick up some wings and pay a visit on good ole Father Ted.

Interlude – A Fable

Fables, stories in which animals act like humans, sometimes even talking, are some of the oldest tales around. Often, they have a moral, teach something or point to a behavior that can be better seen when it is stripped of every vestige of humanity. Here then is a fable, offered as an interlude in our story. Make of it what you will:

A frog found himself in a covered metal pot. The pot sat on a stove (though the frog did not at first know this.) It was dark and warm inside – the frog stretched his limbs on the surface of the water, relishing the radiant warmth that seeped into his amphibian bones. He did not wonder, even for a moment how he had gotten here. It seemed natural that he should float in the delightful, warm water. After several moments errant thoughts crossed his mind. Perhaps it was not natural that he was here? Who had placed him here? Was the water getting warmer? He remembered a story of another frog in a similar situation. A human hand had dumped her in a pot of cold water, slamming a lid down. Fearful of the outcome, she had flung herself upwards, knocking the lid off the pot and disappearing through an open window back to the pond in the woods. She spoke of the incident afterwards. A brush with what seemed like certain death. They eat frog legs, she would often warn her friends.

Perhaps he should use his strong back legs to bounce against the domed ceiling he saw above him, escaping this bath. Could the water be getting hotter? Could the warmth itself be a danger to his life? His natural confidence in his own ability to sense evil was overwhelmed by the sensual delight of the warm water. He knew to the depth of his being that he was smarter than adversity: believed that he knew all there was to know about the dangers of his world. His eyes began to close as he sank to the bottom of the pot. Surely it would turn out okay...

Several years before Moira died, Liam also bought a house in Flour Bluffs, having finally docked his sailboat. He used the money from the sale of his boat to buy a house not far from Billy and Moira, which was also on the canals. This house was a sore point for Luna, since she was still living in a trailer, though by this time she had upgraded to a double-wide. It wasn't long, though, before Liam felt the constriction of living in one place, and since his kids were already young adults, he left again in an RV, "sailing the interstates," as he put it.

It had initially seemed like a good idea to be closer to his aging parents. He had forgotten by now some of the reasons he had left in the first place, and he had been out of the country when some of the bigger changes had occurred with the move to Texas. While he was away, he rented his house in Flour Buffs, making additional income from odd jobs as he traveled.

His skill set was large, including carpentry, electrical work, and mobile home park management. During this time, he developed a persistent cough, which he attributed to a tropical illness he had gotten in his travels, or perhaps his two pack a day cigarette habit. He was suspicious of doctors, a characteristic he had learned from Billy.

Medical care, and even most hygiene to Billy, was "just Madison Ave" – an unnecessary expense designed to separate the working man from his money. Still, Liam noticed that it was getting harder to walk up hills. A return to his house in Flour Bluffs, even for a short while, would allow him to get some free medical care, and though he didn't need the assistance, he was always anxious about money. Perhaps it was time to settle down and take care of himself. With time and distance had come peace; he decided that he must have been mistaken in his unease with Billy. He also felt less of an itch under his feet, and so he returned to Flour Bluffs.

Liam resolved to spend some time with Moira, re-learn his relationship with Billy, and settle into a more mature life. It wasn't long before it was all disrupted. Luna was not happy to have him around.

For one thing, his proximity seemed to make Moira happier. For another, as the oldest son, he carried with him a certain authority that Luna lacked. The Quinns could be very traditional in some ways, and this was one of them. They had often been reminded by their grandmother that in Irish Catholic families, a mother should even go so far as to only count sons when asked how many children she had.

Billy also seemed hell bent on replacing Jimmy's status as an "adopted" son with Liam, his actual son. Worse, he seemed to momentarily forget his anger and resentment of Liam. In fact, Billy now made a point of moving Liam's picture to the front of the plastic holder in his wallet.

"You can just see who the favorite is now," Billy proclaimed. Worst of all for Luna, Liam was more fun for Billy. He had interesting stories about his world travel, and he was always up for an adventure in a canoe or kayak. Luna was determined to set it all straight again.

She began a campaign to "sow some dysentery in the ranks," as Jimmy would say. On trash night, she would sneak over to Liam' house, adding extra bags from her own trash to his pile. Since the community had to pay for trash collection with stickers placed on the bags, and since Luna's additional bags were unstickered, Liam was getting fined for each bag she left.

At first, he was puzzled, and assumed that a neighbor was causing the problem, until he was awakened one trash night by the sound of a car cruising by without headlights. The next trash night, he hid among the bushes, determined to wait all night for the culprit to appear. It didn't take long before Luna pulled up in her battered

Volkswagen Rabbit (lights off). He waited for her to unload two large bags before he came out of the bushes, but he wasn't quick enough. Dashing to her car, she took off at speed for her trailer. By the time Liam ran for his own keys and followed, she was long gone.

Angry, he banged on the door of her darkened trailer, where the Rabbit sat in the driveway with the engine still warm. At first there was no answer. Finally, Jimmy came to the door in boxers, blinking at the porch light. "What's up?" he asked.

"Where is she?" Liam fumed, barely containing himself. When the dull-witted Jimmy hesitated, Liam shoved past him into the bedroom where Luna lay in the dark, a comforter pulled up to her chin. Liam pulled back the quilt, revealing a fully clothed Luna. Jimmy grabbed him from behind. "What do you think you're doing?" he screamed, as Luna shrank into a corner, crying.

As they argued, Luna pulled out a cell phone, calling Billy.

"Liam has gone crazy!" she sobbed, "he's here threatening me."

The fight which ensued ultimately involved the whole family, spilling into the cul-de-sac in front of Billy's house at 3 am. Billy was infuriated that he had been woken up, and even angrier that Liam insisted that Luna was wrong, even when Billy had tried to end the argument with a decisive reminder, "I'm your father."

Several weeks of silence followed. Liam kept his distance from all of them. Then two things happened in quick succession. First, Liam' biopsy report came back with bad news. He had stage IV lung cancer: a certain death sentence. Second, Luna had moved to her next tactic – complaining that Liam had stolen an old dinghy that rightfully belonged to Caster and Poleax.

The *Cirrhosis of the River* was a heavy polished rowboat with teak trim that Billy had originally acquired in Brooklyn for his own sailboat. Just like many things in their childhood, it was never clear exactly how it came into Billy's possession. Perhaps he had traded for it, or just as likely, there was some manipulation or even outright theft involved. Its original owner had perhaps been a doctor whose specialty was treating alcoholic patients, hence the name. The dinghy was last seen sitting on the upper deck of the doctor's large power boat as it cruised through the canal.

The powerboat annoyed Billy for its ostentatious size, fuel consumption, and for the way the doctor reveled in his ownership. He didn't need that boat, Billy thought, and he certainly didn't need that dinghy. Inexplicably, the rowboat disappeared from the deck of the powerboat shortly before another identical green boat appeared in Billy's yard.

After the family made the move to Texas, the *Cirrhosis* made the trip with them. Over the years, it acquired several more coats of cheap green paint, gradually looking shabbier and shabbier until Billy was anxious to get rid of it. When Liam left on his sail around the world, Billy gave it to him as a parting gift. Liam lovingly restored the boat, stripping off the layers of green paint, polishing and sealing the teak underneath, and replacing the fittings with polished brass. On Liam's return to the US with his own sailboat, the dinghy was transformed to its original dark wood and sleek lines. It immediately drew Billy's attention. Though he no longer owned a sailboat himself, it didn't seem right that his dinghy was now Liam's. He didn't need it.

This was the context in which Luna called Liam unexpectedly one evening, just after he had gotten the news about his cancer. He was shaken and trying to figure out how to tell the rest of his family the news. Moira's 80th birthday party was coming up, and Luna had planned a whole family celebration. She had invited everyone, even the Others. Except, of course, that nasty Monica and her family. Liam didn't want to ruin Moira's moment in the sun, but he wanted to share and get some family support. Surely, they would all rally around him, help him with appointments, and sooth his dying days. Moira had not yet gotten her own cancer diagnosis yet, and she was still his mother.

Luna began the conversation screaming.

"How could you?" she shouted.

It was immediately clear to Liam that Luna was playing to an audience on her side of the phone; amping up her hysteria to feed the family drama. Perplexed, Liam assumed that Luna had discovered his diagnosis, and was assuming that he would reveal it at the party.

"Don't worry," he said, "I'm keeping it to myself."

"That's the problem," Luna continued sobbing, "it belongs to Poleax!" Liam paused, confused now. "What are we talking about here?" He asked.

"The *Cirrhosis*, of course! Dada only lent it to you!" she chortled, "It belongs to Poleax! He needs it to go fishing."

This last assertion was especially confusing to Liam. Bizarrely, though all of Luna's children had grown up by the water, none of them had learned to swim. Equally, they seemed to have a horror of anything even remotely related to the sea, unlike the Others, and their children, all of whom swam, fished, and even raced powerboats.

"Dad gave it to me..." Liam tried to say calmly before Luna began shrieking incoherently and slammed down the phone. Liam was determined not to give in on this point. Refurbishing the boat had taken him hours of stripping, sanding, polishing, and refitting. It was a work of art now, probably worth hundreds, as well as a memory of his time sailing.

Several hours later, Moira showed up. When Liam came to the door, she looked at him with an icy stare, one eyebrow raised, a look that all her children dreaded, knowing that it spoke of her resolution along a particular path. "You will give that boat to Poleax" she said, emphasizing each word. "I can't fight about this anymore," she said. There was a moment of silence between them before she turned and walked back to the car where Luna was waiting, a triumphant smile on her face.

Liam' wife, Ramona, would later haul the boat to Luna's trailer, dumping it on the lawn. It would still be rotting there when Moira and Liam were long gone.

Liam was weary. Though he attended Moira's 80th birthday party, he came late, announcing his diagnosis to the assembled crowd and leaving immediately. He visited Moira often as she lay dying, but asked Ramona to keep Billy and Luna and the Spankendopoulos family away when several years later, he was in failing health.

The Others tried to rally around him. Omar Bradley visited with his family, as did Siobhan. Monica came and read one of her son's favorite books to him – *Puddle to the Sea*, a story of a model boat that travels the Hudson to the open ocean. Before the pain got bad, Liam called his own son, Liam III, to his side. "Don't trust Luna," he implored, thinking of things he had seen, "she's evil." Liam III was not convinced, believing the story Luna had told him that his father was delirious on pain meds.

When the Others left, Luna appeared regularly at Liam's door. Ramona was exhausted by now with the daily grind of caring for Liam. Surely it would be okay to let Luna stay with him for a few hours at night. Perhaps it would even be a chance for them to reconcile.

In the haze of his last night, Liam opened his eyes to see Luna by his side. In recent weeks she had become obsessed by a horrible vision. When Liam was gone his wife Ramona would be available. Ramona was older than Liam, and had been a very traditional wife, cooking cleaning and deferring to him for decisions. Though Liam had worked hard, invested, and left Ramona more than enough money, Luna had increasingly worried that with

Moira gone Billy might re-marry, taking Ramona as his wife.

The idea that a father would marry his dead son's wife would seem irrationally salacious to most people, but Billy had provocatively fueled this idea by frequently commenting on Ramona's body and availability to Luna.

"She's a hot one," he would announce to Luna as Liam was dying, fondling the wallet picture of Liam and his wife. Seeing Luna's violent eye-twitching repressed fury only made Billy say it more frequently.

"Maybe I'll marry her right away," he started to speculate, completely disregarding the idea that Ramona would have any choice in the matter, "we could do it right here in the backyard yard." He announced, with a smirk.

Luna had begun to dream of the event. Billy and Ramona standing barefoot on the grass, dressed all in white, surrounded by the beaming Others. They had urged Billy to re-marry following Moira's death, and "spend it all." Luna's plans would be ruined. Most of the picture of the informal atmosphere for the wedding that was conjured up was worse, with all that it implied of the importance of love and relationship over appearances. It was nasty.

Her face contorted, she leaned forward to whisper in his ear. "There'll be no grass wedding for your wife and Dada," she hissed in Liam's ear. "I'll make sure of it."

Liam focused his eyes on the far corner of the room. Moira and his grandfather were standing there, by a glass door that seemed to open to a sandy beach. They were both glowing with a yellow light that outshone the glimmer of the waves. Moira stepped closer, holding out her hand. Liam looked to his left, where a hideous gargoyle seemed to occupy the chair by his bed, its face twisted in rage. Nauseated, he turned back towards Moira and his grandfather.

Rising from the bed with ease, he didn't look back. "Blue waters," he said.

When Fr. Krankenkopfer's file had first appeared on Bishop Garcia's desk, he was concerned. Here was a priest with more than adequate credentials – only middle-aged, which was on the young side for a Catholic priest these days, with a solid set of academic degrees, who had served in nearly a dozen different parishes in as many years. Bishop Garcia was known to his brother clergy for the inordinate pride he took in his profile, which he liked to think of as "Aquiline nose." Privately, he was fond of talking about that same feature as his "bullshit detector." He smelled the aroma of that distinctive fragrance now. Why would Fr. Krankenkopfer move so much? Bishop Garcia knew the answer wouldn't be found in any official file, but there were a few things to consider.

First, if there was an issue like the ones he was reading about in the Boston Globe, who would it really hurt? In Boston, it was Cardinal McCarrick who ended up taking the hit for the shenanigans that had gone on in his diocese, not the bishops. If this priest was a problem, he would be arriving (and maybe departing again) under Cardinal Juma's watch. Juma's problem, not Bishop Garcia's. Second, he needed a dynamic speaker to bring some energy to Corpus Christi. Get some butts in the seats. Fr. Krankenkopfer was known to be a dynamic force in his parishes, perhaps ironically. If he created some energy and buzz, it would only help the case for Garcia's own eventual elevation. Besides, if he asked too many questions, it might come back to haunt him later.

Bishop Garcia signed the transfer order. For better or for worse, at least for now, Fr. Krankenkopfer was his.

Fr. Krankenkopfer arrived several weeks later, viewing his new parish with studied resignation. He had left Milwaukee just in time to avoid any awkward questions, after that Schuele boy had begun to spill the beans. Ted would miss the good German food, but not the weather. Surveying the inside of the mission-style church, he tried not to think about the other things he would miss. It was too early to start thinking of replacements. Were they his prayer group, or his prey group?

He didn't have any remorse for the trail of victims he had left behind over the years. In fact, he never thought of them as victims at all. They had enticed *him,* flaunted their potential to him. Whatever happened later was entirely their doing. If anything, he was teaching them about sin, an important but practical theological concept, and redemption. God's great goodness to them all, he thought, with a cynical smirk.

It wasn't long before the parish had begun to accept him with open arms. Fr. Ted was charming, and even though his short stature and receding hairline did not make him conventionally good looking, his ready smile and charismatic ability to connect to just about anyone made him a natural fit to the diverse parish. In the first few months, he went out of his way to reach out to the neighborhood, showing up unexpectedly to community events, including high school and pee wee football games, and working his way along the sidelines. His ability to listen attentively and make people feel like they were the only person in the world created a magnetic curiosity about the church. It wasn't long before Sunday Mass was growing with new families looking for a connection.

The youth groups, ironically called Pray and Play (a Catholic Youth basketball, and video game group) grew quickly, attracting new members largely by word of mouth. Almost reflexively, Father Ted was able to select from these the ones who were certain to be most available, or most afraid of betraying what would become their secret.

But Father Ted had grown sloppy, an indication, he believed, of his growing weariness with the life of a clergyman. He had been a parish priest for over twenty years, mired at the lower end of a long chain of command, and certain to retire to the obscurity of a monastery or priestly retirement home that did not suit his many talents.

It was time to find an exit strategy, a better route to the happy golden years. When Luna Spankendopoulos arrived on his doorstep, wiggling her ample nether regions in indignation, he had a glimpse of something elusive, a mind just as conniving as his. He wasn't sure where this would lead him, but he was certain that God would provide, and when Luna appeared at his door again after Moira's death (and Greek Orthodox funeral no less!) he already had the whisper of an idea.

Just the Sunday before, he had looked out at his congregation. Luna and the rest of the Spankendopoulos crowd had begun to attend less regularly. He cleared his throat, ready to begin his homily. A fast one, he thought, talking about the Prodigal son. Waywardness was on his mind. A few days before, he had spotted a short item in the local paper, the Bluffs Ledger, announcing a funeral for Moira Quinn at Saint Nicolas Greek Orthodox church. Ted scanned the item quickly, thinking perhaps it was another Moira Quinn, but the details all matched, right down to Luna's name as a survivor.

None of it made sense. Moira and the Quinns were obviously and proudly Irish Catholic, and by rights his parishioners, even though that lame husband of Luna's might have been originally Orthodox. In the days before the funeral, Luna didn't call him either. Clearly, her allegiance was shifting. But he was not a man to be trifled with, and he had too much invested in this now to give up.

It was another item in the paper that really got Ted thinking, this time about the local Catholic diocese, Luna and his next steps. Syrian refugees were coming to Texas. They were Catholics fleeing religious persecution at the hands of Isis. He would have to move carefully, keeping a lot of balls in the air, he thought to himself with a note of whimsy, but he could do it. Picking up his phone, he dialed Luna.

Careful to keep just a note of urgency in his voice, Ted began, "I need to see you tonight," he said, his voice quavering.

Luna resisted – it was raining, and she was frankly done with Ted. He had served his purpose, and now that she had everything she wanted, what use was he anyway?

Ted continued, "Come tonight at 7. One way or another, I have an appointment with the bishop tomorrow."

This was annoying to Luna, but she couldn't really imagine what he might be planning. He had escaped pedophilia charges because of Luna. Anything else he had done, the confessional secrets, the information about Moira, would only hurt him as well. She resolved to go and to dress in the skimpiest outfit she could find, something that showed off her thong, the 69 tattoo, and some cleavage. Jimmy was asleep in his Barcalounger, head titled back, the squeal of tires from an action movie playing on the tv, an oilcan of Fosters' clutched in his right hand when Luna burst dramatically through the front door.

"Wake up," she commanded, shaking him.

"Woz up?" he replied fuzzily, wiping drool off the corner of his mouth.

"That priest from the church..." Luna began, conveniently forgetting his name, "he called . . . wants me to come over . . . tonight."

Luna paused again, waiting for a reaction from Jimmy that wasn't coming. Was he even listening? She struggled for the appropriate emotional note between victimhood and angry indignation. Jimmy continued to stare, lost in the deep fog of beer, sleep and an extra-large blunt. He knew that he was supposed to understand Luna's posturing but wasn't sure it was worth the effort. He also knew she was talking about the church, for God's sake, a trace of amusement creeping into his face at his own pun. Maybe it was a woman-thing crisis, like a bake-sale or something. Jimmy screwed up his face, hoping he looked focus.

"You don't get it!" Luna said, voice rising. She was annoyed that Jimmy was enjoying himself again while she slaved away managing everything. His facial expression, lips pursed, cheeks straining, looked like he was straining during a bowel movement. "What's the matter with you?" she continued, not waiting for an answer. "You don't get it! HE wants to seduce me; a girl can tell." She said with her eye twitching at the idea that Jimmy didn't get her obvious allure. "He wants to take me away from all this," Luna said, gesturing in a sweep that included the Barcalounger and the painting of dogs playing poker on black velvet.

Jimmy might have been lazy but he was roundly inspired to action at the idea that he might lose his gravy train.

"I told you he wouldn't just fade into Boliva!" Jimmy said, his voice rising. "Priests have trouble with that celibacy thing. Not many men could be monotonous like me," he continued.

"Shut up, you idiot," Luna said, shaking her head. "I have a plan, but I need your help."

Without explaining any of her arrangements with Fr. Ted, Luna described the call inviting her to the rectory that night. Father Ted, it seemed, wanted her to come to dinner. He was plotting something, she thought, but she had a different plan. She would wear her most seductive Tuesday Taco night outfit –

"the Hooter's shorts?" Jimmy interrupted.

Luna glared at him, "Bring the video camera. When Ted gets going…film a little bit, then burst in. We'll teach him to go to the Bishop."

"I get it!" Jimmy snickered, "sow a little dysentery in the ranks!"

By 6:45, all was in place. Jimmy was outside the Rectory, a building that he continually referred to as "the Rectum", hiding in the bushes with a video camera. Luna had been sure to find a spot with a clear view of the sliding glass doors to the dining room. Jimmy loved the idea that they were on a secret mission for justice. He had smoked a whole blunt and had several large swigs from the handle of Jose Cuervo that he kept for special occasions. Luna was worried that Jimmy wouldn't remember the steps to the whole process, so she had written them in black ink on the back of Jimmy's hand.

"1) Hide in the bushes,

2) Record the dining room,

3) Burst in shouting, 'let go of my wife!'"

The last bit was a tad dramatic, even for Luna, but she needn't have worried. Jimmy had accidentally spilled some tequila on numbers 2 and 3 and had erased them when he licked off the excess. It wasn't a problem, though, because Jimmy had a mind that he self-described as "like a steel clap." He would remember it all. Luna knocked on the door.

Father Ted's big idea came to him as he was reading about the latest round of refugees trying to escape the Middle East. Syrian refugees were flooding into Houston (apparently a large Arab enclave) to escape the persecution of Christians, which was accelerating with the pressure on ISIS. Here was an opportunity, he thought, to build a discretionary fund for aid under his own control. He would convince Luna to "contribute" some of the seed money, before going to the Bishop with his idea. It would be his penance to build the fund, he would say, turning on the charm. When the funds had grown enough, he would empty the account, and disappear into the wind.

Why would Luna contribute? Because he would tell her that it was her penance, and an important step in preventing him from taking his knowledge of her schemes to the rest of her family, or perhaps the authorities. He wouldn't need much, perhaps $50,000 of the money she had gained. A small tax, really, on her large windfall.

Ted could hear the doubt in her voice when he called. A crack in her usual confidence that she had him under her thumb. Over the years he had learned that the best ideas came with a whisper of his intuition – that voice that told him what lay ahead. *Deo Gratis*, thank God, he knew it wouldn't fail him now. When Luna rang promptly at 7, he was certain that his instincts were right on target. She must be quaking in alarm.

Opening the door, he was shocked at what he saw. Luna was dressed in tight red satin short shorts, a strapless gold spandex top that showed off both her midriff and her tattoo, and white plastic boots laced up to above her knee. This was not the quaking housewife he had imagined. This was a black widow on patrol, looking for a replacement for that goofy husband. Priding himself on his ability to pivot, Ted waved her into the living room, reaching for a bottle of cognac.

Outside, Jimmy was already bored. He tried to focus on setting up the camera and remembering the steps beyond 2. It was dark, and it was uncomfortably hot. He settled himself against a tree trunk and began to drift off. Years of practicing at his county job had taught him how to find a good place to lean for a quickie nap.

Inside Luna was re-assessing. The shimmering light in Ted's eye, the cognac, the night meeting. Yes, he definitely wanted her – even more than the day when she had given him the lap dance at the picnic. She knew she could manipulate him, but why not have some fun as well? From his vantage point, Jimmy couldn't see them. A quicker wit might creep closer, looking for a more secure view, but quicker he wasn't. She could indulge for a few moments before moving to the dining room for the final act.

Outside, Jimmy had defied expectations, creeping all the way into the house in time to see Luna mount Ted's lap, red shorts cast aside on the floor, head thrown back, eyes closed. Jimmy stood in the shadows of the living room doorway taking it all in, camera forgotten. This was way better than his favorite video series, *Game of Bones*, better even than *Add Momma to the Train.* When the tryst had reached a noisy conclusion, Jimmy crept back outside to his spot by the tree, camera off. Let Luna find him this way.

Inside Luna and Ted mentally circled each other, each trying to decide what came next. Luna was surprised to find that she didn't really want to end this night dramatically. Perhaps there was more here than she thought. Ted was not by any means good looking. Older and bald, many would have said he was "dumpy." At the same time, Luna loved the idea that she was controlling him, working him into a state of desire. Perhaps there was more here that she had originally guessed.

Ted too sensed an opportunity. Luna was a sex-starved middle-aged woman, though she imagined herself to be an alluring high-level school administrator with her hooks in every man she encountered. Though he also did not find her particularly good looking or attractive, her years of hard tequila drinking and careless disregard for self-care had made her have a hard edge that was unappealing. Still, there was also something about her availability and longing for solace beyond her dim-witted husband. Ted's taste ran more in other directions, but here was a chance for gain, if only he pressed the right buttons. He was certain that he was much smarter than Luna. A few years of careful management and he would be able to have it all, anyway: the money, the interim pleasure, and the exit strategy.

Outside, Jimmy had gone quickly back to sleep under a tree. Luna was relieved when she glanced outside and didn't see him. Plans had changed. Ted's idea about milking Liam, hiding the money, and running away to Italy made sense to her. She would use Ted to escape Jimmy, hide the money from the Others, and start a new life. Of course, once she had escaped, she would blame it all on Ted, and disappear for good.

Gathering herself, she shook Jimmy awake. "Did you see it?"

Jimmy pondered for what he hoped was a short minute. If he said yes, he wasn't sure if that was good or bad. Would Luna ask him if he had it on tape? What would he say? He vaguely remembered that there were things he was supposed to do and say, but what were they?

Luna dabbed dramatically at her eyes with a balled-up tissue, eyeing her stupefied husband. In a flash, she understood: Jimmy had forgotten the instructions, and had fallen asleep out here. Too much tequila and pot, as usual. She resisted the impulse to hit him hard in the ear as she usually would.

With a rattling inhalation, she continued, "Fr. Ted helped me to see it all. I understand finally why I'm here – why we're here – what we're called to do!" She paused, sizing him up. Was he even paying attention? She dabbed a little too energetically at her eye again, accidentally poking herself and provoking an actual tear.

"It's the Liberians," she continued, unsure what actual group Ted had mentioned, "they need our help!"

Jimmy was used to hearing things that confused him. Truthfully, most of the world confused him. Still, this was a new one. Luna plowed ahead, "we're going to donate money to the Liberians. Father Ted, bless that holy man, will take care of it all."

Jimmy may have been confused, but this didn't sound good to him at all. They finally had gotten to the point where that irritating Moira would stop interfering and now, they were going all holy? What about his new double-wide, with a man cave and mini-fridge?

Luna didn't want any push back; he could see it already. Her eye was twitching. Never a good sign. "Tomorrow we'll write a check for the Algerians," Luna continued, already forgetting which country they were donating to in the delicious excitement at the power she was wielding.

Billy didn't need to know right now. As for Jimmy, he was like a baby who was distracted by jingling keys. They would spend this weekend at Ted's house. Jimmy would lounge in Ted's jacuzzi, drinking his tequila. Luna would work Jimmy up a bit but slip him a roofie. When he was safely tucked away for the night, she and Ted would play. It was exhausting keeping all of them -- Ted, Jimmy, Billy, and her kids - occupied while her plans unfolded. It was a good thing she had thought of the plan with the Albanians to hide the money for a while.

Bishop Garcia was irritated that Fr. Krankenkopfer was on his schedule again. In the days following the newspaper revelations about his disgusting little escapades, Bishop Garcia had to do a lot of damage control. First there was the mother of the victim, who annoyingly pushed the idea that Krankenkopfer needed help, that the church needed to open its records, and "explain to the public what it was doing to protect the youth of Corpus Christi." Here Bishop Garcia caught the unmistakable whiff of pride, an aggrieved mother, and worst of all lawsuits. Luckily, Krankenkopfer had somehow persuaded that "Luna" woman to being the smiling face of complacent Catholicism, staving off any bad press by appealing to her position as an educator, and consequently, a great judge of human character. The settlement offer put quietly forward by Father Esposito, his canon lawyer, hadn't hurt either. The family would move, at the Church's expense, to a larger house on the other side of Texas. The son would enroll in the local Jesuit school, and all would be forgotten in the purifying fire of an NDA, and a large check.

Garcia had hoped that Krankenkopfer would disappear as well, moving on to retirement or leaving the clergy. He had been surprised that Krankenkopfer decided to stay, and even more surprised to see him here now. Garcia watched as he crossed the large room that doubled as his office, spreading his shabby Cossack around him as he settled across the desk like a Southern Belle awaiting her next dance partner. Garcia waited in what he hoped was a stern yet prayerful silence for Krankenkopfer to begin.

"On prayerful reflection," Krankenfopfer mumbled in what he hoped was a suitably humble tone, "I believe I have much to offer in the way of penance, and more, that will please your Grace." Here he paused, waiting for some gesture of eager anticipation from the

Bishop. Sadly, there was none. Bishop Garcia was an old hand at negotiation, and his aquiline profile smelled more to come. Better not to tip his hand. Not to appear too eager.

Krankenfopfer went on, "a wealthy member of my parish would like to establish a fund, to assist the refugees from Syria. These monies," he paused again, dramatically dabbing at one eye as if overcome at the generosity of it all, "would be held in an account at the IOR..." Bishop Garcia snorted loudly, stunning Krankenkopfer into silence.

The Vatican Bank, also known as the *Instituto per le Opere di Religione* (IOR) was the internal financial arm of the Vatican. Religious organizations within the church, Garcia knew, could deposit funds into accounts there with a Bishop's approval, and then use their deposits as collateral for large interest free loans. It wasn't a conventional bank, in the ordinary sense of the word. There was little in the way of oversight, and much in the way of freedom. Powerful men controlled these accounts, often re-directing some of it to gain even more power. Krankenkopfer was an idiot, Garcia thought, if he believed that he would let him come within sniffing distance of an opportunity like this. Besides, Garcia thought, scowling, he was giving Krankenkopfer just enough rope to sink himself and Cardinal Juma too.

"Impossible!" Bishop Garcia said, perhaps a tad too loudly. "Parish priests do not control such accounts. Why not set up a parish fund, and have your parishioner contribute to it?"

"I don't think you understand," Krankenkopfer continued, daring a smarmy smile. "These are my funds. Solicited and maintained by me. I can understand your reluctance, since we don't know each other well," another smile, "but Cardinal Juma is sure to be delighted, since he is himself Syrian, I believe, and more than that..." Krankenkopfer paused, "there is much for you to gain in the long run. Have you ever heard of Mar Elian?" he asked.

This was a trump card, a nudge that Krankenkopfer had held close in case he had to use it. He wasn't an educated man, in the church sense – not given to the finer points of theology, liturgy or canon law – but he had a finely tuned intuitive sense that had told him to bring a couple of little wedges to shove into any cracks in the Bishop's veneer.

His research had told him that before being relegated to the relative backwater of Texas, Garcia had spent a decade as the Prefect of the *Biblioteca Apostolica Vaticana*, or the Vatican library. His sudden, swift transfer out of the library and out of the Vatican to America suggested a secret that was an opportunity for Ted. He vaguely recalled a scandal at the time -- something about manuscripts disappearing. Perhaps the Bishop would be open to the idea of acquiring some early church manuscripts to sell for himself.

Bishop Garcia's pause spoke volumes, Krankenkopfer thought, with amusement at his own pun. Garcia was staring at him, mouth slightly agape, as if he had paused in mid-sentence. He waved his hand to continue.

"Mar Elian was the first of the Syrian monasteries to be burned by ISIS, in their ongoing war against the One True Church. It was reported in the press that they viewed the scriptorium with hatred, since it contained books that they considered blasphemous. Soldiers reportedly entered first to scrawl slogans on the walls, and then urinated on the books before pouring gasoline on the piles and setting them afire."

Krankenkopfer thought that perhaps he had gone too far. Bishop Garcia was looking pale, and his hand was hovering by the bell to ring for his assistant. Was he genuinely distraught over the waste and historical loss this represented, or was it, as he suspected, another loss he grieved? Krankenkopfer had filled in the blanks of Garcia's biography with the belief that the transfer had occurred because the Bishop had been a little too fond of the manuscripts, perhaps stealing some to pad his own retirement account. It was this theory that fueled Krankenkopfer's offer to Garcia.

"I met a young man," he continued, speaking rapidly before Garcia decided to throw him out, "who was once a lay brother at the monastery. He is here, a refugee from the troubles in Syria. He has knowledge of manuscripts that survived. Important manuscripts." This last phrase was uttered in a confidential whisper. Garcia's hand returned to his lap.

Krankenkopfer could see that he had struck a chord with the mention of manuscripts. Garcia did indeed love early church documents, but not for the reasons that Krankenkopfer imagined. Nor had his banishment from the Vatican grown from a self-serving interest in them. For many observers, Garcia's exile was just punishment for a sin that they would see as not too different from Krankenkopfer's: falling in love with a young Scriptori. The truth was far more complicated.

Mgsr Giacomo Venturi was almost the same age as Garcia when they first met, but his ready smile, long delicate fingers, and intense way of listening made him a favorite of many of the Vaticanista. As Prefect, Garcia, who was also a Monsignor at the time, was technically Venturi's boss, but their many easy confidences soon made them close friends. It was Giacomo that first made Garcia think about St. Peter.

"There is a revolution happening in the Catholic church," Giacomo explained. "As the last vestiges of authority weaken, and the dominant culture leaches in, many things are changing. None of us," Giacomo continued, "can resist the pull of a culture that is so intimate, so pervasive, much longer. When we take a hardline position, when we insist, gesturing in a circular motion to those around them, that they meet us here, we lose every time. Change is inevitable, and we see it as a threat to who we are," he lowered his voice and continued rapidly. "It doesn't have to be – it doesn't have to threaten our identity, sweeping away the best of what we have here. We can meet them where they are, invite them in so to speak," he said, his eyes lighting up.

Garcia was mesmerized by Giacomo's passion, and by the truth of what he was saying. Giacomo had paused:

Garcia prodded him, "How?"

"It is said that nature abhors a vacuum," Giacomo continued, "and while that is not strictly true, it is an apt metaphor of where we are – a mask, if you will, of the truth. Change is not only destructive of the old, but also an opportunity: a chance for a new beginning. And" he said triumphantly, "most new beginnings arise from a seed that germinates from what is already there. We have our seed – St. Peter, the original rock."

Garcia understood immediately that Giacomo was referring to the disciple of Jesus, a flamboyant firebrand originally from Syria, who Jesus had renamed Peter (Petrus, Latin for the "rock.") Perhaps the most loyal apostle, ready to fight to save Jesus' life, the gospel also featured prominently stories of his later cowardice in denying the Lord three times, and his remorse; qualities that humanized him and made him more accessible to the masses. His activism in the early church was also well known, along with his eventual journey to Rome to become the Bishop, and thus the first Pope. His life followed a trajectory parallel to Christ, including running afoul of civil authorities, and a crucifixion death. (According to legend, however, it was performed upside down, a humble denial of his alignment with the death of Jesus.)

Garcia also knew that several recent Popes had longed to re-connect somehow with the example of Peter, in the hope of renewal. This had largely taken the form of searching, apparently fruitlessly, for the grave of the Apostle beneath the Basilica of St Peter. Finding the grave close to the seat of modern power, it was believed, would

143

bestow a final note of legitimacy on Mother Church's waning authority. Pope Pius XII himself, it was said, would appear nightly at the excavations in the crypt, staring mournfully into the hole, praying for a positive outcome. This couldn't be what Giacomo was talking about since the Vatican had moved on from this idea. Before he could ask, Giacomo continued.

"Peter was known to be a prolific writer of letters, sermons, and even books. Most of them were written though before he came to Rome and the originals lay outside the Vatican Library, many in Syrian monasteries. The power of faith for us," Giacomo said, thrusting a finger empathically towards the table, "has always resided in the stories which guide us. Here was a man who knew the Lord himself – who lived on to guide the early church towards a closer union with Jesus. All of this," Giacomo said, again gesturing to the Vatican around them, "the hierarchy, the rituals, even the prayers, is just a mask for the that relationship, a pointer towards the truth."

Settling backwards as he reached a conclusion, Giacomo continued, "the younger generation understands this – they live in the context of many stories of their own creation. That's how we must reach them. With the power of a narrative that drives them back to the person of Jesus. It's there, I'm sure," he added emphatically. "In the Syrian monasteries. In the unknown writings of St. Peter."

Not long afterwards, Garcia had gone to his superiors. He confessed his growing attachment to Mgsr. Venturi, and asked, humbly, to be released from his Prefect position. The Cardinal was puzzled by his honesty, especially since there were few in the Curia who would not act on those feelings instead of requesting a transfer. In affection for Garcia, it was arranged that he should assume the post of Bishop of Texas, a backwater sure to keep him out of trouble. A few days later, without saying goodbye to Venturi, Garcia left Rome.

Krankenkopfer interrupted the long silence, shifting in his chair. Garcia thought, landing this manuscript would be a coup indeed, as well as an opportunity to return to Rome, and reconnect with Giacomo. As Garcia had gotten older, his departure from Rome and Giacomo had become one of the biggest regrets of his life. Over the years, Garcia had followed Giacomo's rise through the ranks at the Vatican Library. He had also come to be content with his feelings for Giacomo not as a potential sin, but as the deepest form of companionship. Such a manuscript would fulfill Giacomo's dream for his career, and it would also allow them to reconnect; to be re-united in their purpose of "making all things new."

Krankenkopfer coughed discretely, continuing, "The refugee I located has access in-country to manuscripts belonging to the monastery, which were rescued before it was burned by terrorists. Some of these are previously unknown works of St. Peter."

Here he paused, waiting for a reaction to his statement. Garcia waved him on. "We can use the Syrian refugee fund I propose to acquire these works and bring them to Rome." "Finally, the point," thought Garcia.

"A few questions, Father." Garcia said, holding up his hand to stop Krankenkopfer. "What assurances do we have of the provenance of these documents, and indeed that they are what you purport them to be? Further, why should we not simply work with this gentleman through normal channels?"

Krankenkopfer smiled, noting that Garcia was referring to himself with the royal "we," and thinking of a famous joke that ended with the punchline "What kind of girl do you think I am? And the answer...We've already decided that. Now we're just haggling over the price." He knew that he had Garcia's attention, and that now he only had to reel him in.

"The simple answer, your Grace, is that you have to trust me, at least for right now. I have a plan that will allow us to gain further evidence without incurring any expense to the Church, using funds that I have already raised. If it is not as promised..." here Krankenkopfer shrugged, "there is no loss to any of us except wasted time."

Garcia sat back, his elbows on the arms of his chair, fingers tented under his chin. Krankenkopfer pulled a completed document from the leather portfolio that sat on his lap, recognizing with the instincts of born salesman that he had to pounce to close the sale: the paperwork necessary to open a bank account at the IOR, which required Gracia's signature.

"I have taken the liberty of preparing the paperwork for your signature," he continued, thrusting the papers forward on the Bishop's desk.

Luna and Jimmy had been paying regular visits to Ted's house during the years after Moira's death. Often, they would spend the weekend, with Ted making a lavish dinner, Jimmy soaking in the jacuzzi, and smoking weed afterward. It was always good to get away from the drudgery of his regular life and to let someone else tend to Luna's many demands. Jimmy always made a point of retreating to the guest bedroom early, falling asleep with headphones on, watching porn on the bedroom TV. Luna and Ted used the time equally as creatively, enjoying the idea of danger at Luna's husband resting nearby. When playtime was over, the two would plan their next moves. It was during one of these pillow-talk sessions with Luna that an argument started.

Luna was tired of contributing money to the refugee fund. She needed to know what was in it for her. After all, she was a woman of the world. She understood tax write-offs, she said, but surely there was enough money for that already. Besides, what would they do when the old bastard finally died? She wanted out from that dimwit Jimmy and her children. The twenty years spent caring for them was enough. There was no longer a need for what they provided: a perception of who she was, and a vehicle for making demands of her parents. What then?

Ted sighed heavily. He had to placate Luna, certainly. She was an interesting diversion and, let's face it, a useful cash cow, but she was also a dangerous enemy. The story he told had to contain enough of the truth that she would be satisfied, lulled even, but not enough that she could find him afterwards. "It's a long story," he began, watching closely as she settled in to listen.

"We have to find a way to move as much money away from your family, and your siblings…to hide it and preserve it. Then, when the time is right, we'll leave with it, start a new life somewhere they'll never be able to reach us." Here he paused, contemplating the right emotional note to strike. He was aiming for somewhere in between jealousy and fear. "Remember that Omar Bradley and Monica will work together to destroy you, if possible. They hate you, and they'll use all the resources afforded to them by their glamorous lifestyles to make sure that they get what's rightfully yours."

Luna's eye was already twitching. "Go on," she said, listening.

"So, let's work backwards," Ted continued. "Where can we go that they can't ever make us leave?" he paused briefly before answering his own question, "we have to find a country where we can live well, have access to all of our funds, and where (this is important!) there's no extradition treaty with the US, so they can't arrest us and send us back. The answer is the Vatican City!" he said empathically.

Luna looked at him skeptically. "Go on," she said impatiently.

"The Vatican is a sovereign state," Ted continued, "a historical vestige of the Papal States. It has its own government with a sovereign head, including cabinet ministers and laws, and it has its own bank. Unlike other banks, the Vatican bank is not subject to any outside regulation. Its sole shareholder is the Pope, and it is answerable only to his Holiness. The catch is, though, we can't just set up an account there. The only deposit accounts at the bank belong to religious organizations, accepted on the approval of a bishop, and they are set up to provide collateral for interest-free loans for some special humanitarian purpose. That's where the Syrian Refugee fund comes in..."

"I get it, I get it," Luna says, annoyed at the long story, "we're essentially laundering money, and we can escape there, but why should the Bishop want to help the Syrian Refugees?"

"Let me finish," Ted says, annoyed himself. "It has to do with a bit of Church history. The original Pope was St. Peter. There's even a kind of joke in his name; *Petrus* in Latin means "rock" and when Jesus renames him, he calls him the rock on which the church will be built…"

"Who cares?" Luna says, twisting Ted's nipple hard.

Ted smiled, enjoying both the idea that he was making Luna impatient, as well as the thrill of sharp pain.

"We do," he continued, "because Peter is the key to change in the church. Even though Peter was the first Pope, much of the theology of the early church was founded on the writing of the Apostle Paul. For a while now, the larger culture has been drifting away from Holy Mother Church, and the Vatican has been scrambling for ways to draw people back. Beginning even before World War II, they have been convinced it has something to do with St. Peter. In fact, several Popes looked for his grave hoping to re-establish that connection, but…"

"I'm going to hurt you if you don't get to the point soon," Luna said, squinting. Ted thought deeply for a moment. "Is that a promise or a threat?" he said with a smile, before continuing.

"The point is, in Syria, there are a bunch of really old monasteries. St Peter was Syrian, and if any place might have some of his other manuscripts, it would be there. A Peter manuscript would be an authoritative source for theology that might help us find a new direction. In fact, for several hundred years at least, they have been hinting that they have some undiscovered treasures. Now ISIS has overrun some of them. They burned several monasteries down, but not before some of the manuscripts were rescued and hidden by the faithful." Ted again paused, hoping she was getting the point. Luna glared at him.

"The Bishop knows all of this. I went to him and suggested that we set up a Vatican bank account to rescue Syrian refugees. I also told him that I could get access to those manuscripts and bring them to Rome. He knows that I'll need the cover of the Church to do this. I'll need access to cash and false travel documents, among other things. He also knows that whoever might find such writings would wield enormous power in the Vatican and would be sure to be promoted to Cardinal. That man would ultimately be a force to be reckoned with in the next Conclave. I told him that the rescue fund would be my penance; that I was willing to walk away at the end and leave the glory to him. Of course, you and I would also escape. Flee with our new passports and a boat load of cash to Vatican City, and then disappear. The Bishop wouldn't look too hard for us, because it would be better if he never saw us again, and as for your aggrieved relatives...do you really think any of them have the resources to chase us around the globe? We'd be free." He paused again, studying her face.

Luna stared at the ceiling, lost in thought. She would let Ted hide the money, get the passports, entertain her for now, and plan their escape. When the time came though, she would take it all back and disappear herself, leaving him to wonder what happened, and most importantly, to take the blame. She smiled again as she turned to face him. "It'll work," she said.

In the immediate aftermath of Moira's death, Billy had basked in the sunshine of attention lavished on an elderly widower. As time went on, reality took hold. Moira had been the center of the family, easing the way to almost anything Billy desired. She reveled in the company of her children and many grandchildren and delighted in their accomplishments. During the years after leaving Brooklyn, she had begun to travel to visit many of them for family vacations, or to join them for some event. Billy tolerated these excursions, but he never really liked them: they were not fun *for him.* Increasingly as the years went on, he pushed back. He needed to stay in Corpus Christi to take care of the Spankendopoulos kids.

Partially, this was because he was falling more deeply under Luna's control: she had him "tied in knots" he said, and she "wouldn't take no for an answer." Moira too had given up trying to hang on to her autonomy. It was too exhausting to argue with Luna. If they disagreed and Luna felt she hadn't won, she would leave the field of battle and get right on the phone to cry to Siobhan, Liam, or Omar Bradley. (Monica had long ago broken off contact and trying to call anyway would usually result in Bella Notte hanging up on her.) "The parents were too much," Luna would sob, "what should she do?" Billy and Moira both increasingly had only the illusion of autonomy. There was always a Spankendopoulos around to "help", or report back.

When Moira was gone, so were all the illusions. Managing Billy was a whole family project and the Spankendopoulos clan was in it to win it. Billy was isolated in his home. Luna took over his care, and his bank account. Caster and Poleax moved in to "help" him, but there never seemed to be food in the fridge, or clean sheets on the beds. They took his car away in fear that he might drive. Jimmy gave it to his daughter, Clamydia. They turned the ringer down on his phone so that he could nap in peace and erased his messages so he wouldn't worry. Now and then they trotted him out for large family occasions, being careful to clean him up beforehand, and to seat him somewhere that would make it hard for him to hear to limit conversations. He lay in bed day after day, feeling the loneliness, and the accumulation of years, and listening for the sounds of the kids tiptoeing out of the house with his knick-knacks. They'll steal anything that's not nailed down, he thought. He drifted in a daily haze watching the light on the ceiling.

Luna had been slightly unmoored by the rapidity of his decline. She remembered that pigs had been an important part of Billy's metaphoric universe. He liked to talk about politicians as being "mere pigs at the trough," or that anyone in the family who was selfish (read: not going along with what Billy wanted) was falling prey to the "pig philosophy."

Now, though, Luna was reminded of another of Billy's pig metaphors: "Pigs get fat, hogs get slaughtered." Fr. Ted had warned her about moving too fast. It was important to transfer the money slowly, bleed it off through gradual gifts, and not rush to grab it all overnight. The Others were still out there, and though they weren't interfering now, it might only be a matter of time before something she did got their attention.

The first big move came just before Moira died. Luna told Billy he had to be careful. Omar Bradley was a lawyer, after all. He wouldn't do what Billy wanted! He kept talking about *Moira's wishes,* as if that mattered. Billy was scientific. They should do a test. Let's tell him, she said, to change the will. Liam should be written out. After all, he was dying. What would be worse than seeing all their hard-earned money going to Liam's wife and "half-breed kids?" "If he's on your side, if he's your lawyer, he'll do it," she urged.

Predictably, Omar Bradley refused. "It is not only wrong," he said calmly, "it is a conflict of interest since any diminishment of shares would benefit me in the long run. Do what you want," he continued, "but find your own lawyer."

Billy was secretly delighted by the drama of Luna and Omar Bradley fighting over him. At the same time, he remembered the cold halls of St. Joseph's orphanage, and his bitterness that there was no family willing to care for him. Blood was all that mattered, but it had to be blood that did what he wanted, that was loyal to him no matter what. Luna found a lawyer to change the will, but not before they made another small change. This time, Siobhan was in her sights.

Luna invited the entire family for a Thanksgiving dinner at her double-wide. Billy offered to host it at his house. It was larger, he said. She could cook anyway. No, said Luna, wiping away a tear. We'll do our best (cheerful long-suffering smile.) The truth was that Billy hoped that hosting Thanksgiving would force Luna to clean his house. It was quickly sliding into disorder under the supervision of Caster and Poleax. Luna was adamant, though. Billy could even see her eye twitching.

On Thanksgiving Day, Siobhan arrived with her whole family. Her sons had stayed in Connecticut to have the holiday with their respective in-laws. During the appetizers, Siobhan circulated pictures of her middle son Michael's new house. It was a sprawling multi-room McMansion in the suburbs of Connecticut: an easy commute to his job as a stockbroker in the city. Billy glanced anxiously at Luna, whose eye was beginning to twitch. Siobhan was meanwhile oblivious, reaching over to her husband Mike to pat his hand affectionately. This was too much for Luna, whose eye moved from twitching to full-on convulsing. *That smug bitch* she thought, dropping a tray of cheese balls deliberately to recenter attention on herself.

On the way to the new lawyer's office, a few days later, Luna made sure to underscore the picture to Billy. "Siobhan doesn't care about you anymore," she said. "Her husband and sons are millionaires. If you die, they'll get her whole share. More pigs at the trough," she said for emphasis. Billy wasn't completely sure. If he wrote out Liam and Siobhan, there was no reason for Luna and her dim-witted husband not to take it all before he was even dead. He would appease her by meeting her half-way – he wouldn't write out Liam, but he would create a poison pill. The legacies to the Others would be smaller, eccentric amounts, designed to make each of them look at each other and wonder why the other got a different amount. Siobhan would get the smallest amount of all, so she would resent both her own family and her siblings.

It was a lot to manage, but Luna consoled herself with weekend excursions to visit Fr. Ted. Jimmy was always content to go along, happy to drink and smoke himself into a stupor (or so it seemed to Luna.) She continued to donate lavishly to Ted's stupid Assyrian fund, or whatever, knowing that eventually she would be able to leave the country with him and start over without Jimmy and the rest of the idiots. Meanwhile, she made that naughty Ted work for his shekels. As long as it was fun for her.

The rest of the money slowly moved to the Spankendopoulos kids as gifts: a car for Clamydia, a condo for Zooy, trailers for Caster and Poleax, and a large sum of cash left in the will to Oozy, since she was still a minor and under Luna's control. Meanwhile, a steady stream of checks drawn on Billy's account were written to pay for vacations, clothes, and upgrades to the Spankendopoulos double-wide. These checks were a sweet lullaby of greed designed to mesmerize Jimmy and keep Luna happy until it all ran out, or Billy died, whichever came first. But then, Billy started to lose it.

It was in early spring, almost six years after Moira died, that Billy began to decline. The house had by now been emptied of most large or valuable objects, the last items were Monica's childhood piano (an instrument she never wanted, since she played the oboe, but which Billy had insisted she should be grateful for) and Omar Bradley's grandfather clock (his first large purchase while on duty in the Army.) Billy had woken up one morning to find the piano missing. Disturbed, he called Luna.

"Where's my piano gone?" he demanded.

Luna had never liked the piano, as it represented all that was wrong in her present life. First, Moira had liked to arrange pictures of the grandkids on it, for all to see when they walked in the house. At least, some of the grandkids. There were pictures of Monica's two sons, one a brilliant surgeon in his white coat, the other a highly sought-after consultant for major corporations posing casually by a restored fighter jet (his current hobby.) There were also pictures of Siobhan's three handsome, successful sons and their families, as well as Liam' two smiling children, also sailors. And of course, there was a picture of the newest grandchild, OB, jr. playing baseball. The only ones missing, of course, were the five Spankendopoulos kids, to be added, Moira said, "if they ever accomplished anything."

Then there was the fact that it was "Monica's piano." If anything made Luna's eye convulse, it was that nasty Monica, with her glamorous New York apartment, her hussy of a "wife", and their degenerate lifestyle. Luna had two of Jimmy's goofy friends take the piano while Billy was sleeping and donate it to the church. The pictures all went in the trash. Luna didn't want to admit it to Billy, but what would he know, anyway?

"What piano?" she answered, denying everything.

Billy was sleeping more and more. He was calling Monica and Siobhan at odd hours to complain that he was all alone, that he couldn't find his glasses, that he hadn't eaten, and that he didn't know what day it was. Luna thought it was all too much. Why did she have to take care of everything? She had a career, and a family to think about. They should put him in one of those nursing homes! Jimmy was quick to remind her that Billy's pension was almost $3,000 a month. He liked having the extra money for his weekly trip to Hooters, and he liked the Billy ATM that paid for anything his little leeches wanted.

And then Siobhan's oldest son, Dermot, stopped in to visit Billy during the day when Luna and the twins weren't around. He found an emaciated Billy, his hair shoulder-length, with fingernails long enough to make an exotic dancer proud, laying in a darkened room in a stupor. The sheets were filthy and smelled of urine, and Billy was staring at the ceiling. Billy wasn't sure for a moment who Dermot was, though Dermot had always been one of Billy's favorites.

Dermot helped Billy to the shower, cut his hair and fingernails, and ordered groceries to be delivered. He was serving Billy sardines on toast when Luna came in, screaming as she entered, "what do you think you're doing?"

Dermot blinked. Luna had always been one of his favorites, more like an older sister than an aunt.

"I cleaned him up," Dermot said, getting angry. "How could you leave him like this?"

It was then that Billy seemed to understand that they were fighting over him, usually a delightful idea. He looked at Luna waiting for an answer.

Her face contorted in rage she screamed, "do YOU want to clean his shitty diapers, asshole?" pushing Dermot out of the room as she yelled.

Luna immediately called Siobhan. She wanted no more drama. No more visitors. DaDa couldn't take the selfishness of it all.

Four days later, Billy was found on the floor unconscious. The hospital said his age was catching up to him, as he was 97. Luna wailed continually when others were around in a crescendo of pre-grief. To Luna's dismay, Billy was transferred back home for his final days of hospice care.

By now, there were few to attend Billy's dying days. Siobhan came with her husband, of course, but they were chased away because they were "too nosy." Omar Bradley had been banished when he refused to help disinherit his own brother. Monica too had been banished, though she often called late at night to talk to him while the hospice nurse put the phone by his ear. Liam was long dead. Over the years beginning with Monica, each of the Others had been pushed to the periphery of their parents' lives. Each of the Others too accepted these exclusions: it was easier to believe that there was a good reason for this, than to accept it was deliberate and based on lies and manipulation.

Monica may have been the first but after all, she was openly gay and defiant. Liam had a yearning for travel, and when he finally returned home, he deliberately antagonized Luna. Omar Bradley was an advocate for Luna, had "boundaries" and was not a fan of Luna. He refused to be manipulated by Luna or Billy. Siobhan had the advantage of distance, and the confidence to ignore slights and odd behavior. Perhaps her awakening to the reality was the most painful because it was the slowest.

And then there was Moira. Billy had imagined that she would return to him in his final days to offer comfort, to ease his way ahead, but Moira was long gone. The room was often empty, except for the nurse. Luna insisted on keeping his morphine dose low, because she was concerned about addiction, she said. The truth was that she needed to keep him around as long as she could. There was still money left, and time was running out.

On one of his last days, he drifted into a hazy memory of a sunny day, surrounded by family, all of them doing what *he wanted*. They were having a meal and talking about an elderly neighbor who had recently passed away in a nursing home. Billy felt smug at the time at the idea that he would avoid a nursing home, and that he would be surrounded by family on his last day. Then Liam was telling Billy that at the end of their neighbor's life, the man's son had refused to see him, as he was dying. They all laughed. Billy began to cry.

He could just make out the nurse nearby, and Jimmy standing in the doorway watching. He could feel his bowels begin to loosen, and he stretched out his arms towards the bathroom, begging for help to get there in time. The nurse looked at Jimmy, "I can't get him up alone. Can you help me?" Jimmy stared for a long moment, as if he hadn't heard. Billy remembered that he had told Liam and Omar Bradley on Luna's wedding day that he had another son now, Jimmy. He thought of all that he had given Jimmy over the years, the ways he had helped him. "I'm not hurting my back for him," Jimmy said turning away.

Billy turned his face to the wall. *Why don't they just put me to sleep, like an animal?* he thought. He remembered seeing an overworked horse shot when he was a child, and various pets put down over the years. They slumped into death with evident relief. He had no regrets of things left undone, relationships not nurtured, or things unsaid. Increasingly, in his state of immobility, he noticed with annoyance that some people were not as interested in him as they were before. They didn't seem concerned that he might take something away, or not give them something they dearly wanted.

He drifted into a hazy vision of the tile-lined hallway of St. Agatha's Orphanage, opening from a vast room lined with empty iron beds. The room was dark with little light filtering through grimy barred windows that lined one wall. Billy began to walk down the hallway towards a distant sunlight window at one end, partially open to warm summer air.

Billy could hear the voices of children drifting in and could smell the brine of the oceanside. He smiled as he walked closer for a better view. Improbably, there was a beachfront outside, where lawn should have been, with bright white sand leading down to a softly rolling surf. All his children were there, playing noisily along the water; each of them as he remembered them from childhood. On some level, he knew this was the antidote to the cold emptiness pulling at his back but seeing his children in the sun only made him cringe into a deeper loneliness.

Long ago, when he was a boy, one of the foster parents had taken him to St. Patrick's Cathedral for a Sunday Mass. Even then, he hadn't believed in any of it. "The Sun God is my God," he would tell his children, aiming for the provocative.

"Religion is for the weak and the perverted. It's like Karl Marx wrote in his *Communist Can of Pesto*," he would say to his kids, "religion is the dopiate of the classes."

In the Cathedral, Billy had turned his eyes up, tracing the lines of the arches overhead. At the crux of one of these arches, he spotted a gargoyle, its face twisted in a snarling rictus, one finger pointed down at him. The face haunted his nightmares for years. Now, he turned back to the center of the room at the sound of voices. The gargoyle was staring down at him again, screaming,

"DaDa, wake up. Don't go…"

Billy recoiled into the darkness.

Interlude – The Others

"The black sheep is sometimes the only one telling the truth." – Anonymous

You may well ask, Careful Reader, why there is an interlude here? The answer lies in the character of the Others themselves, who were peripheral to the story for the simple reason that one-by-one they had learned the truth, as painful as it might have been: they had bought into a lie. Their family hid behind a façade, a mask, if you will. At its core was a single poisonous lie – a myth of connection.

The truth, much more painful to face, was that the legacy of Billy's childhood of trauma was a cancer that slowly eroded all the relationships in the family. Each of the Others found it hard to believe at first, and still later each would assume that they were the only one who were targeted by Billy or later Luna, and who were isolated and cast out. It was a long cycle of recognition and grief, and since each of them came to it gradually, it wasn't until very late in the whole process that they were able to bond together to try and stop it all before it was too late.

It was then that Omar Bradley called a meeting in Chicago.

Omar Bradley arranged a dinner meeting in his hometown of Chicago. The meeting took place at his favorite restaurant, a themed barbecue place on the Loop called *Lord of the Wings*, not far from his office. Monica and Siobhan agreed to fly in for the weekend, to talk it all over without their spouses. It was long overdue, they all thought, and fitting. Moira capped every celebration with a meal, often at a special restaurant. This was a celebration of sorts, though not of a life event. It was a long overdue recognition of what they really were: survivors. It was also a strategy meeting. They all liked the idea of implicitly invoking Moira.

Their meal was served in a party room at the back of the restaurant, far from the boisterous activity of the mid-week after-work crowd. The main dining room thumped with a bass track that they could hear like a heartbeat from the back, as they ate their wings and made small talk. Omar Bradley had asked that they wait until they reached the dessert course before talking seriously. They had the room for three hours, he said, and the staff knew him well.

When the waiter had left them with coffee and cake (tea for Siobhan,) they began. Omar Bradley proposed they talk for a few minutes about what they had each noted over the years, before moving on to what's next. Siobhan offered to speak for Liam, since she had been closest to him in age. Monica started.

"To a certain extent," she began, "I'm confused by what happened. My family was on the outskirts of the family a long time, but I always assumed it was the gay thing. Mom and I had made peace over that. She visited us, came to graduations, confirmations and stuff...Dad was different." Monica paused, sipping her black coffee with an ice cube.

"Dad manipulated everyone with money and acceptance. When he called to ask us to come to some event in Texas or at Siobhan's in Connecticut, it was always with the implied threat that if we didn't come there would be some consequence. Not that he ever gave us something, but he would chime in with that stupid Shakespeare quote about the bed. Tic is another story, but she's supposed to be a younger sister. I only heard from her when she wanted something or was spreading some gossip that seemed calculated to stir the pot."

"Mom was something different," Monica continued. "I thought when she died there would be a legacy for my sons, or possibly one of the rental properties for a retirement house. Remember, they never helped us buy a house, something they did for all their children, and even some grandchildren, and I had given Dad money as a down payment on one years ago."

She paused, stirring her cup, "again, I assumed the gay thing. But since Mom died, I learned how much Tic manipulated both of our parents. Liam thought Tic was evil and he told me stories about some of the stuff she did..." Monica's voice trailed off.

"Anyway, I like what Omar Bradley says about not letting her steal our future. Bella Notte says that Luna is a sociopath. At first, I thought saying that was overly dramatic but then I did some research...There are a lot more of them among us than we thought. They are hard for us to see because they make us complicit in their decisions and *they look just like us*. In this case, they're family. They are charming, she said, speaking carefully. They know how to manipulate people to get their way – anything goes, even manipulating other people's sense of reality." Monica paused, watching their faces.

"Think about it," she urged, "a sociopath has no conscience. Anything goes," Monica said emphatically. "Nothing ever stands in the way of what Ticv wants, not the law, not relationships, certainly not any ideals. The important thing to remember too is that Dad was like this too once. He opened the door and Tic walked through." They were all quiet, thinking.

Siobhan spoke for Liam. "Ok, I'll speak for Liam first," she said with a sigh. "Remember that he moved to Flour Bluffs when he became ill. During the last years of his life, Luna worked hard to torture him with stupid little gaslighting tricks like leaving extra bags of trash on his lawn that she insisted were his, and bigger things like insisting that he had stolen a dinghy boat from Castor and Poleax." Monica and Omar Bradley were nodding silently, remembering.

"Dad was dead to him long before. There were things that happened back in Brooklyn that made him afraid of what Dad was capable of" Siobhan continued,

"Liam was not surprised by anything that Dad did, no matter how malicious it seemed, or how manipulative. Luna was more of a surprise. He had been away long enough that it was startling how evil she was. That's the word he used," Siobhan said. "It made the last years of his life more miserable than they had to be. And Liam was really afraid that his own children didn't believe him about Luna."

Turning to Omar Bradley, Siobhan said, "SHE even tried to convince Liam that you wanted to poison him. "

Siobhan continued, "For myself, when Monica didn't show up at family events, I believed what Dad told us…that she was too busy living her glamorous New York lifestyle, that she hated men, that she wasn't interested in the rest of us because we were too working class, and she was a scientist."

Siobhan paused, shifting in her chair, "but then Liam was dying, and he called me and told me all this…he also said that he saw Jimmy erase phone messages on Dad's phone, saw Luna throw out cards from Monica, overheard other people talking about the lap dance on the priest's lap. There are too many incidents to remember, but it amounts to this: now I see clearly that Luna worked hard to manipulate and isolate Billy, all for money."

"Dad told me that he knew in the last days of his life that Luna and Jimmy would have been nothing without his money and his support. He called them failures who were an embarrassment."

Siobhan stopped, looking at Omar Bradley. "In one way, the money doesn't matter, it never did. What matters is that we all lived with an image that was a lie. We believed that we were safe in the family. That we were fair with each other; supportive of each other. If you think about what the idea of family meant to Dad in the home, and where we are now…it makes me nauseous. That's what Luna really stole from us." Siobhan stopped.

There was silence as they all thought about the events of the last several months since Billy had died. Cousins were at first perplexed by the obvious tension among the Quinn family. Then, the eyes of various relatives were opened. They had all witnessed moments when Luna clashed with each of them, always asserting her need to control.

Everyone at first told themselves that she was doing all she could to protect Billy, out of an excess of devotion. But then they saw clearly how much Billy seemed to be lavishing gifts on only the Spankendopoulos family, to the exclusion of everyone else. And they saw the disdain that the Spankendopoulos kids had for Billy, how they treated him as a slightly eccentric cash machine. They saw how Jimmy and Luna dismissed Billy or ignored him over and over in private, saving their lavish praise for the more public family events. The last straw was the funeral.

Billy was in a flimsy "transport" coffin, for shipment to a free veteran's cemetery in the northeast. Luna talked the funeral director into putting Moira's ashes in a coffee can in the same box. The burial featured a stop for bagels at a drive-through afterwards, not a family dinner or reception. With all the money they had now, everyone was aggrieved that Luna couldn't even spring for a few hundred on lunch. And then the will: Luna got it most of it – including the rental houses. She was also the executor of the little money that was left: a perplexingly small amount, since Luna had bragged to Liam's daughter when she was drunk that there were "millions" left. Everyone started calling Omar Bradley.

They all believed that since he was a lawyer, Omar Bradley would have a way to stop her. The money left behind was not important to any of them. Each of them had made their careers. But at the same time, they were all frustrated at the lopsided way what was left was distributed.

They had learned that money was a vehicle for manipulation. Surely, they believed, at the last there would be equity among them. Yet, the bulk of everything went to Luna, including a long list of "portable property" that went to Spankendopoulos grandkids, even when it should have gone to one of the Others. For the first time too, they all saw that while much of Billy's behavior was odd or manipulative, Luna's was far worse. She had alienated each of them one-by-one from Billy, controlling everything about his care, draining his bank accounts, and ultimately grabbing what was left.

Omar Bradley looked at his siblings, "are you finished?" They both nodded.

"I wanted us to meet, face-to-face to explain a few things," he paused, gathering his thoughts. "Since the will came out, everyone has been calling me – grandkids, great-grandkids, even Liam's kids. Everyone is asking the same thing – 'can't you do anything?' 'can't you sue?' As if it's that easy! You have to have a case." He paused looking at them.

"There. Is. No. Case. He let Tic control it all – let her take everything. All those phone calls you made to him mean nothing. Your thoughtful gifts, visits, pictures…NADA. She was 'Teacher of the Year', she was an attentive child and most important, he put it all in writing. Ironclad. There's nothing else to do."

Siobhan interrupted. "But she abused him and manipulated him. She robbed him blind and took all that money. What I really don't understand is, she's still living in that trailer with that Knuckleoplois guy. Where did it all go?"

Omar Bradley sighed, "I told both of you when Mom died that this would happen. No one believed me; no one wanted to do anything. You trusted him, and that meant you were trusting Tic. As to what she did with the money, she gave some of it to the Knuckleopolis kids. I suspect that the rest of it is somewhere we can never touch it. Someone helped her hide it. And when the dust settles, she'll leave them all behind – maybe retire with the lap-dance priest. The both of you, and everyone else left in the family, need to set some boundaries. Don't call Tic, don't talk about her. Block the bitch and forget about her. You think it would upset her if you filed a lawsuit? It won't. She loves it. Feeds off of it. Walk away. Dad left us with a legacy for sure – a legacy of distrust. Walk away."

Siobhan broke the silence. Turning to Monica she said, "you say she's a sociopath, and it's not that I don't believe you…I just don't understand. How could she have fooled us all this time?"

"You keep thinking we're a family, but it's more like a cult." Monica said, "Let that sink in and think about this. Imagine I told you about someone who set a fire, burned a barge down, and set his son up to take the blame? You'd say he was an arsonist and a sociopath for involving his son. Imagine someone who routinely stole things from other people because 'they didn't need them' and gave them to other people? Or a daughter who manipulated and isolated an old man, her father, who stole from her siblings…you get the idea. We all agree that the things Tic and Dad did show no conscience, so your other question is, why don't we see it? Why didn't we all say long ago that she is a sociopath?" Monica paused before continuing.

"It's too close. You know her, and you will use any other explanation in the book before calling her what she is. She's just like you, except...There must be another reason. Blame her and you have to believe that evil can live right here, right now. You missed it all along."

Omar Bradley was nodding. Siobhan was overwhelmed and silent. The evening was over.

Part Five – Meals on Wheels

"Vengeance against predators is meals on wheels." Stefan
Molyneux

*"Loose ends can never be properly tied, one is always
producing new ones. Time, like the sea, unties all knots."*
Iris Murdoch

After the meeting in Chicago, the idea of stopping Luna from completing her plans was essentially closed. Looking back, the Others thought of all that had transpired as pathetic. Their father, one of seven children raised in orphanages and foster homes, longed for family. To him, the idea of a family life was the primary goal. His children all absorbed his ideal, but with a distortion: an image in a mirror. Over and over, they had been manipulated in their lives, pushed to conform to whatever values Billy insisted were right, even as his behavior was different; to attend family events at any expense or inconvenience with little reciprocity, to excuse any strange behavior or accept any lies. Rules for Billy were mutable; for everyone else they were unbreakable.

The legacy of trauma from Billy's childhood was radioactive; seeping through the generations in half-lives to infect the children, some grandchildren, and almost no great-grandchildren. Ultimately, though, his biological descendants would continue. His legacy was distrust, anger and fear of each other. It was a zero-sum game.

After Moira died, each of the Others looked back and questioned the things they had believed. Still, each never questioned themselves about the many things they had believed about each other. Did Moira have an affair and threaten to leave Billy? Was Monica really a "man-hater?" Who told them that Liam' children were "maybe-babies?" Why did Siobhan marry so early? Did Monica really refuse to come to Moira's 80th birthday, or Billy's 90th? The source of each story was always either Billy or Luna.

As Billy's health declined, each of them also believed that when the end came, they would all see that he loved them all equally, as a father should. They believed that he wanted them each to bond with each other, to carry on a legacy of family love and solidarity into the future. The message would come the way he had always sent them a message: with a gift that he left them, a share in the fortune that Moira had made. If nothing else, they believed that his last word would not be a gesture towards further distrust among them.

The grief began when it became clear that that wasn't true. Not over money, per se, but over the lopsided, heavy-handed way that Luna was allowed to accumulate it all. Not just his attention during his lifetime, but lavish gifts of everything he owned of value to her children, and then most of the money and property that was left after he died.

Even items of household property went to the Spankendopoulos crowd, including many knickknacks that Moira had collected in a lifetime of travel, childhood gifts from her own children, Christmas tree ornaments and vintage appliances from their first home. Luna also didn't hesitate to create a new manipulative narrative that resulted in Billy disowning both his sons, several grandchildren, and leaving a tiny inheritance to Siobhan who had encouraged the backyard "grass-wedding" that Luna had predicted would occur between Liam's widow and Billy. Liam had been right: Luna was evil.

Recognizing Luna for who she was meant one thing only: walking away. She wouldn't stop, couldn't stop, because the psychic energy of the destruction she left in her wake was the only vitality she could feel. Every one of Billy's children was as isolated in their own way as he himself was when he stood on the threshold of the orphanage, waiting to encounter the larger world.

The Others didn't mourn Billy's passing, because he had instilled in each of them a lasting bitterness for the harm he had caused, and the relationships he had fractured. They weren't angry at the loss of cash, or property. They were hurt by all the illusions that were finally shattered; the masks that had been ripped off.

Still doubting, each of the Others had reached out to lawyers, hoping to find there was something they could do. Each of them heard the same thing: you will never win.

171

She's Teacher of the Year. She's been planning this all along, and has every step aligned. It will cost you too much money to be worth it. Where's your proof? Then, they each remembered their resolve at the *Lord of the Wings* and moved on.

Once upon a time, every family gathering had ended with a group photo: Billy and Moira at the center, surrounded by an expanding array of children, spouses, grandkids and great grandkids. Surely the passing of the patriarchs should have been a liminal moment; a final gathering and a glimpse ahead. Yet only Luna's family and a few cousins attended Billy's funeral. Monica and Omar Bradley stayed away. Siobhan came with her husband, leaving immediately afterwards. No one thought to take a picture of the few that were there because it didn't matter anymore. They turned their backs and walked away. There was no photo.

Fr. Krankenkopfer also made plans to move on, after six exhausting years of placating Luna and Bishop Garcia. There were many overseas trips to Syria, careful transfers of money from the IOR through a maze of Byzantine offshore accounts, along with meetings to arrange a series of new passports. He was moving slowly, he told Bishop Garcia, to make sure that he had hold of the manuscripts with no chance of repercussions. Bishop Garcia was only mildly impatient. Garcia understood that Krankenkopfer would come up with the goods, or he would have to explain how he spent all that money. Either way, Garcia would be rid of him.

Keeping Luna at bay was more difficult. She longed to move on, away from that dim-witted Jimmy and her leech children; to show the Others who was finally boss. Every weekend she asked Ted when she could leave with him. The pressure was unrelenting.

When the will became public knowledge, Liam's two children were shocked and unhappy, but no one else expressed any real surprise. "It figures," Monica said, with a shrug of her shoulders. "I told you so," said Omar Bradley. Siobhan had been the last to believe and was still grieving and disbelieving. This was a disappointment to Luna, who had secretly relished the image of herself as the dutiful daughter victimized by her grabby siblings.

Krankenkopfer knew that he had to finalize things before the end of the Probate period for the will. It gave him three months after Billy's death to get ready for the escape hatch. He set a date with Luna when she should meet him. They couldn't leave together, he explained. She would come by his house, pick up her new passport, documents, and a plane ticket, then go straight to the airport to get on the plane. "Don't tell anyone," he reminded her, "and be careful how much you pack. Leave all your other IDs and credit cards at home, or better yet, get rid of them. Just get on the plane. I'll meet you on the other side," he said with a smile.

On the day they had planned, Luna drove to Ted's house, letting herself in with a spare key. She had a small bag packed with some of her cutest outfits. The new documents were hidden under his statute of the Blessed Mother, just as he said they would be. There was an Italian passport and driver's license under the name Perfetto Pompino, the combination an Italian slur that amused Ted. Luna frowned. She hated the name and was confused by the Italian passport. Wouldn't she have to speak Italian? Ted had left a cheery note on a pink post-it on the front. "See you there! Terminal by the exit" it said. There was also a ticket to Rome on a flight leaving in two hours. She would have to hurry to make it on time.

Seated on the plane, she tried to focus on starting over. Jimmy would be confused by the note she had left. "Gone to Mexico," it said, "starting over. Don't look for me. Goodbye." Ted had told her not to leave a note, but she couldn't resist the drama of poking at that dim-witted Jimmy one last time. She had followed the rest of the instructions, shredding her passport, credit cards and driver's license and setting fire to the pieces in Ted's fireplace. Arrivederci, Flour Bluffs, she thought.

When Jimmy found the note, he was not as distraught as Luna expected. Tossing the note in the garbage, he grabbed a beer from the fridge. "Time to retire," he thought, settling into his chair in his man cave. Luna had been exhausting, and not anywhere near as hot as she was when she was younger. The truth was that he was relieved that she was gone. For years he had been saving overtime money, stealing from Billy himself, and hoarding it all up for his own eventual escape. After a nice dinner, a little weed, and a few beers, he would leave in the morning himself with that nice young waitress from Hooters. Time to finally say goodbye to this stupid town.

174

Luna may have thought that she was getting the best of him, but it was all good. Like his mama always said, all of the chickens come home to toot.

Ted had left the night before, driving himself to the airport and checking in to a flight for Rome, before changing clothes in a bathroom and walking back out to grab a taxi into town. From there, he walked to a train station, and bought an overnight ticket to Chicago using a new set of documents. He took off from O'Hare the next day, having changed documents and appearances again. He wasn't worried about anyone pursuing him. Bishop Garcia would happily blame him privately for the theft of the refugee funds, a substantial chunk of which had landed in an offshore account through a series of complex wire transfers. The church itself would likely do an institutional shrug, preferring to keep its losses private. Ted had enough to live on for now, and would claim the rest later, after a suitable waiting period.

Luna would be furious. Ted delighted in imagining her eye twitching. His one regret was that he wouldn't be there to see it. Now she would have to go crawling back to the Quinns and her husband. The Quinns were not a worry to him. He had covered his tracks though, just in case. They would be more interested in getting Luna than in finding him. In any case, he was on his way to Morocco, a country without an extradition treaty with the US. He would stay there for a year, just in case, before collecting the rest of the money and becoming a ghost somewhere more suited to his refined taste.

Several hours later, Luna arrived in Rome, breezing through Customs. She stood waiting by the terminal exit impatiently for over an hour. How dare Ted keep her waiting? She would make him pay when he showed up. Finally, she gave into the inevitable, and considered her options. She had a burner phone with international service, a new passport and identity, and enough cash for a few months. That Jimmy should step up and send her some more! How dare he think that she didn't need it? Dialing Jimmy's number from memory, she waited.

By now Jimmy was in his truck with his Hooter's waitress, Amber. They were headed to Las Vegas for a few weeks of R&R. First thing in the morning, Jimmy had sent an email to his boss saying that he was retiring. He also crossed the street to his neighbor's lot and banged on the door of his trailer. When the neighbor, who had never been fond of Jimmy, opened his door Jimmy came right to the point.

"You can have it all," he said, gesturing at the double-wide, "for $10K. I'll take a check."

The neighbor, who had endured years of the Spankendopoulos family and their questionable taste, agreed immediately. He had just enough in his retirement account to cover it. Afterall, he could easily sell just the trailer for that price, or it rent it, or even tear it all down.

Jimmy glanced at his phone as he was driving. He didn't recognize the number, but he suspected it was Luna. Amber was fixing her make-up in the mirror.

Picking up the phone, Jimmy barked, "yeah?" Luna was confused. Jimmy didn't sound distraught or at all nervous about where she was or how she was reacting.

"Jimmy?" she asked.

The sound of Luna's voice caused his gut to wrench. In seconds he considered his options. By the time she got back from wherever she was he would be long gone.

"Wrong number," he said, ending the call and blocking the number.

In Rome, Luna stared at the phone. To her left, an elderly American had just emerged from security. He was all alone, balancing several large suitcases on a luggage trolley, and talking into a cellphone balanced under his chin.

His drawl was thick as he said, "y'all don't worry about me…I'm fixing to spend a few weeks traveling and seeing stuff now that Emmy Lou is gone. I'll be just fine."

The man ended the call, looking indecisively around. Luna's intuition prodded her. He was tall, with a full head of silver hair. Though he looked a bit disoriented at the foreign airport, he had the vibe of a man who knew what he wanted. Several pieces of designer luggage were balanced on the luggage wagon in front of him. He stopped a moment, pressing the toe of one snakeskin boot against its edge, as if posing for others to enjoy the view. She could just see the edge of what looked like a fat money belt protruding from the waistband of his tight jeans.

Stepping forward, Perfetto Pompino approached him.

"Scusi?" she said tentatively, remembering the single phrase of Italian she had learned on the plane, "*Da che parte fino al posteggio dei taxi?*"

He glanced at her smiling, eyeing her tight-fitting top and just visible.

"Sorry, darling. No sprecho…"

Perfetto continued stepping closer and bending down strategically to adjust her own suitcase, "are y'all from Texas? Small world! Me too! Can we share a cab?"

Things were looking up for the man already, so to speak.

"Well, howdy, darling," he drawled, smiling. "I'm Hank. It would be my pleasure."

Taking his arm, Perfetto stepped into the Roman sunshine.